Shadowfall

Greg McWhorter

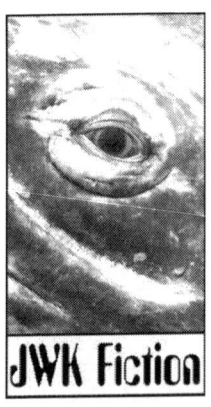

Book © 2016 James Ward Kirk Publishing

Novel © 2016 Greg McWhorter

Internet: jwkfiction.com
Twitter: @jameswardkirk
Facebook: James-Ward-Kirk-Fiction

ISBN-13: 978-0692683699
ISBN-10: 0692683690

Cover art by Jorge Avina. Layout and additional graphics by Jonathan Kittleson

All rights reserved. No part of this book may be reproduced in any form or by any electronic or mechanical means, including information storage and retrieval systems, without written permission from the publisher or author, except in the case of a reviewer, who may quote brief passages embodied in critical articles or in a review.

Dedicated to KAM

For too many reasons to list.

Too bad it didn't last.

Prologue

Germany
May 2nd, 1945

The two remaining officers, still in uniform, looked at each other in silence, neither one knowing what to say. They had their orders to follow. These men both knew for a long time the war had not gone well and feared this day. Without sharing a word, they instinctively knew what they must do.

Within a few hours, not a shred of evidence would remain to suggest that a secret base had once existed within this remote hillside. The battalion of soldiers stationed here would not be missed as they were carefully selected for this secret operation, and were expendable.

With all evidence removed, dismantled, burned, or obliterated, the two men stood facing each other in front of where the base had been. They had already blown up the main entrance to the base. Both men had now put on civilian clothing; all traces of who they were had been destroyed. No nods were necessary as both men simultaneously produced their issued Lugers and counted to three in unison. At 'three' they both fired and killed each other. Their bodies lay in the open wilderness, ultimately decomposing in the lonely forest, unless devoured by wild pigs hungry for carrion.

Shadowfall

Chapter One

London, England
Today

Alfred Armbruster had just sat down with a packet of crisps to enjoy some BBC comedy. His lonely and unkempt flat was dark except for the warm glow coming from the old television screen. Being an ex-lorry driver, Armbruster had always been thrifty with his money, as he could not wait to retire and do nothing. Even though his TV was old, it still worked, and that was good enough for him. He didn't care if it was a flat screen or not. When it dies, then he'll upgrade. For now, as a new pensioner, he wanted to live as cheaply as he could so his money would stretch into his old age. This living cheaply is part of the reason why there was no longer a Mrs. Armbruster. She had left him several years ago, was now living in Essex, and had a new life as a councilman's wife.

He sat quietly with the exception of the crunching noises produced from his crisps. After about an hour of telly watching, he was starting to grow tired. He kept watching TV anyway. Many were the nights he would fall asleep in front of the screen until he managed to wake up enough to drag himself to bed so he didn't care how tired he got. His eyes were getting blurry when he first noticed something odd. At times, depending what the image was on the screen, he noticed what appeared to be dust hovering in front of the TV. At first, this meant nothing to him other than he felt that maybe he should dust his flat in the morning, but after a while, the dust seemed to gain a peculiar definitiveness.

Even though he was feeling sleepy, he tried to motivate himself. For some nagging reason, he felt a dread coming over him as if he were somehow in danger. He sat up a little and tried to focus on the dust. *Am I crazy?* He thought the dust was starting to resemble a human form –a man! He sat and watched for at least an hour as the dust took a slight and crude shape that resembled a man, but nothing else happened. Alfred finally gave up and went to bed thinking that he must be so tired he was dreaming what he thought he saw.

Armbruster woke up early the next morning, decided he was tired of being so lazy, and concluded it was time to clean his flat. Alfred dusted carefully, threw out trash, vacuumed, wiped his TV screen, and even cleaned the grime off his small windows. He was done by the time the morning paper finally arrived. Alfred Armbruster was very 'old school' in that although he had a computer, he still relied on his paper copy of The Times for his news. Alfred didn't quite trust the internet and felt most of the news on it tainted by twenty-somethings who wanted nothing more than for his generation to go die and leave them all their money to squander.

Alfred sat down and read the paper. He was meticulous in studying the paper as he had little else to do and noticed an unusual story buried on one of the back pages. The story recounted how several people near the center of London were complaining of strange apparitions. They all agreed that it appeared dust was coalescing into figures of what seemed to be men. None of those interviewed could give any particulars. They all agreed they were vague apparitions at best, but what was intriguing to Alfred was the number of witnesses that were coming forward. It was not just one or two drunken sailors, or a housewife in the midst of hot flashes, but entire families.

His interest quickly waned as a Manchester United match was about to take place and he put the paper in the waste bin and turned the telly to the football match. Alfred thought no more about his own apparition and went on about his usual schedule for the rest of the day. As night approached, Alfred carried on with his usual routine. He finished making and eating his dinner and then sat in his favorite chair with a snack while tuning in some comedy show. As with the previous night, he stayed up late watching the programs until he became drowsy. Even though he had cleaned and dusted that morning, he noticed that the annoying dust was back again.

Alfred watched carefully this time, with more interest. He now remembered the article he had read and wondered if he were having a similar experience. Maybe there was a ghost haunting his flat? Instead of staring past the dust to view the TV program, he focused on the dust. At first, the dust seemed to coalesce into a figure that appeared humanoid, but it was static; it didn't move. He watched the shape for quite a while until it appeared to be slowly moving toward him! Not knowing what to do, and with that sense of dread stronger this night, Alfred got up and quickly made for his bedroom, leaving the TV on behind him. He locked the door and lay in bed until he fell asleep, unsure of what else to do.

The next morning, he felt a bit sheepish as he walked into his living room. He looked around, but saw nothing unusual, except for his television still on. He turned it off and made breakfast. *Do I have a ghost or am I seeing things?* After eating, he decided to turn on his computer and look online to see if there were any new developments with others seeing ghosts like in the article yesterday. He went to Google, typed in "recent sightings and ghosts," and did a search for only news from the last week. To his surprise, dozens of people across London claimed to be seeing strange "ghost" or "dust" men in their homes too. Most of the articles claimed that a shape, or in some homes several shapes, seemed to be appearing, but they did not do anything. In the most recent articles, however, people mentioned the shape or shapes moving slowly.

Alfred had read enough. He had never been superstitious, nor had he ever been scared of ghosts or ghost stories, but for some reason his senses screamed 'danger' at him. Alfred felt unsure what to do and decided even though he did not truly believe in ghosts; he might call some others in to see what they can figure out about this phenomenon. Doing a quick search of the internet, he found a group called the Greater London Investigators of the Paranormal. On their webpage, he found a 24-hour hotline number and called it. To his dismay, he got a recording. He left a message explaining his apparition and asked that someone come around to check it out. He left his phone number and address. He put down the phone and went on with his day.

Shadowfall

All day long, he rather hoped to get a call, but none ever came. Night came and he fell into his chair with a snack and television, like usual. He had forgotten all about dust and ghosts. Some bills had come in the mail that he had forgotten about. His mind was preoccupied with his meager bank holdings. How to pay the bills without emptying his entire account? He had some bottles to recycle and a few friends owed him some money, but not in amounts big enough to cover all his bills. He may have to let one or two of the bills default into next month and then attempt to catch up on them. He was so engrossed in thoughts of money that he barely watched his comedy program and did not notice the dust that was collecting into a form again.

He finally noticed the form as it was much more distinct tonight than on previous nights. He strained his eyes to stare at it and he determined that it was the shape of a young and fit man! As before, the figure did not move at first, but the more it developed, the more he noticed it moving toward him! *I am not scared of ghosts! They cannot harm the living!* He watched in rapt awe as the dust and shadow figure approached him, slowly. The figure stopped just in front of him and he squinted his eyes at it. *Oh my Lord! It cannot be!* This was his final thought as the ghostly image reached a hand out and into Alfred's chest.

Chapter Two

Gareth dialed the number and let it ring almost ten times before hanging up. He was used to cranks calling and figured this may be another one. The recorded message from the man he was trying to call back had come in yesterday during the late afternoon. One of Gareth's assigned duties was to listen to the phone messages daily and respond to ones that seemed legitimate. As Gareth cradled the phone receiver, he decided he would try back later and give the guy one more chance to pick up the phone.

"What's the matter, Gareth? You look confused. Or maybe frustrated?" Tam said from behind her laptop screen.

"Oh, it's nothing. Just a guy named Alfred Armbruster called and sounded so serious and urged us to call right away and now there's no answer. We seem to get that a lot around here, people pulling our chain, so to speak. It gets so I never know who is being sincere or not. I guess I'm just getting cynical."

"Well...Don't let it disturb you too much. We get all sorts of weirdos calling us. We had almost eleven calls yesterday morning that all sounded a little vague. Eleven was actually a record for us though."

"Yes. I know, but this man sounded very earnest and detailed. He didn't sound like a prankster. His experience was different from the normal that we usually get. Not the wispy ghost thing or furniture moving. He said something about a figure materializing from dust."

Tam pulled her laptop screen down on the table in front of her so she could see Gareth and scrunched up her face in a quizzical expression. "Okay. Did he say anything else?"

"No. Just that he was seeing a ghost made of dust and it was bothering him. He also left his phone number and address."

Tam clicked the laptop closed in front of her, looked at Gareth with a smile, and asked, "Is it close by?"

"Why...Yes. It's ...just a few miles south of us."

"Okay. Let's go down there."

***

Ever since Gareth joined Greater London Investigators of the Paranormal, he had hoped to spend more time with Tam. Seeing Tam in action; investigating an old and reportedly haunted abbey, had made him want to join in order to get to know her. Tam excited him from his first sight of her.

He had been watching television with his mother when a variety show came on. This one featured mostly odd and eccentric people and the various activities they were doing. This particular episode had a segment on modern ghost hunting. The show interviewed Tam and followed her and the team members about as they set up their equipment; monitoring for strange happenings. Gareth could see how passionate Tam was for supernatural investigations. It was seeing this strong drive within such a beautiful girl, about his own age, which excited him. Her easygoing, but enthusiastic nature on the show, her sparkling blue eyes, her golden hair, and athletic build just made her perfect in his eyes. He decided right then to become a part of her team so he could help her with her passion...hopefully in more ways than one.

He had recently turned twenty-three and was a hopeless romantic at heart. Girls made him nervous and he had no idea how to proceed with Tam so he just spent as much time helping her as he could. Tam appeared completely oblivious to his desires, and, in fact, she was.

Tam liked Gareth as a colleague, but she had never thought of him as anything more than that. Tam was not interested in finding love, only ghosts. Ever since Tam was a little girl, she believed her senses were acute and she often felt she could see things others could not. She was very imaginative as a child and had several imaginary friends. As she got older, she felt they must have been the ghosts of other children who were bored and wanted a companion that could see and hear them. To her, investigating the paranormal was what she was destined for and never even thought seriously of dating men. Now in her twenty-sixth year, she felt more love for ghosts than any man she had ever met.

Almost four years ago, Tam, and some of her friends had pooled their resources and created the Greater London Investigators of the Paranormal as a means by which to fully realize their love of ghosts and ghost hunting. Some of the members also prided themselves as being amateur detectives; ferreting out the histories that accompanied each sighting. Others thought the Ghostbusters movies were cool and wanted to live out some kind of movie-inspired fantasy. Whatever the case was for each member, GLIP had acquired a lot of equipment and members in a short amount of time. This helped to keep some funds coming in as each member paid dues. They also got a little media attention whenever there was a ghost sighting or a new horror movie came out. Tam and the others reasoned that even bad press could be good so they didn't care what the media thought of the group and responded eagerly to all enquiries.

Tam and Gareth left the small gardener's shack the GLIP rented behind the same set of flats where most of the members of the GLIP lived. The 'Shack' as they called it had been totally refitted by GLIP members, although it looked like a common gardener's shack on the outside, the inside had been hung with drywall, painted and had new electrical wiring put in. It also contained several thousands of dollars worth of technical apparatus. The building also boasted a thick metal door and several bolt locks.

Together, they crossed the bricked backyard into the lower level apartment rented by another member named Simon. Simon was one of the original members who helped to start GLIP. Simon was the same age as Tam and had gone to school with her. They were old friends and when Tam came up with the idea to start GLIP, Simon was one of the first she told her idea to and made him join. After all these years, Simon was still not sure whether he truly believed in ghosts or not, but Tam's fanaticism was always so infectious that he quickly found himself a charter member.

As Tam and Gareth walked into the kitchen from the backyard, they caught a quick flash of a young man as he walked stark naked through the front room. They both froze in place and looked at each other.

"Was that...?" Gareth started to ask.

Tam answered before he finished. "Yes. That was Simon." They both looked again down the short hall toward the front room. Simon popped his head around the wall with a horrified look at the two, concealing his body behind the wall.

"Ho! What the Hades are you two doing barging in on a chap that's just stepped out of his shower? Tam, you know I've asked you a million times to knock before using my flat as your personal tube station!"

Tam smiled at the thought she must have frightened Simon. Inwardly she reflected that maybe Simon believed she was a ghost coming to check up on him, but the truth was that Simon was just being modest and valued his privacy and hated loony girls barging in on his tranquil bliss. Gareth felt sympathy for Simon, but he knew he could not help himself from following Tam's lead, even if it meant mortifying a colleague.

"Sorry Simon! Gareth and I are on a hot lead for GLIP and we need to borrow your car. We only need to go a few miles and we'll be back right away."

"Hang on a tick. Let me grab a towel at least," Simon said from the other room down the hall.

In a minute, he joined Tam and Gareth. Simon was tall and lanky with black hair and brown eyes. Gareth noticed that he had the types of muscles that were from working out. Maybe Simon was big into sports, Gareth thought. Simon and Tam hugged and exchanged some quick pleasantries before she repeated her request to borrow his car.

Simon seemed to melt as easily around Tam as Gareth did. Gareth noticed this and it made him decide to stay a little distant from Simon's friendship in case they became rivals for Tam.

Simon had looked serious at first, but his expression changed to an airy smile. "Okay. Keys are on the stand by the front door. Please be quick as I need to go out in about an hour to visit my mum." With that, Simon's head disappeared behind the wall and a door could be heard slamming shut about a second later. Tam quickly ran into the front room, headed for the stand, grabbed the keys, and headed outside with the faithful Gareth in tow.

The trip was quick and it was easy to find parking with Simon's small green Mini. Even though his Mini was from 1996, it was in great shape as Simon kept up on all the fluids. It still looked new as he also washed it regularly. Tam and Gareth quickly made for the appropriate residence number and knocked several times to no avail. After their third attempt at knocking, an elderly woman wearing a stained apron stuck her head out of a window nearby and yelled out to the couple.

"Tha' man's gone! He has leff' fer good. Be away wit ya'!"

Tam looked over at the woman and said; "Do you mean he has moved? He called us just yesterday and left this address."

"Nay, woman! He has passed through the Veil. His body was chust removed. Now stop knocking on tha' door!" The woman withdrew her head, closed her window, and drew her shades.

Tam looked back at Gareth. "Well that ends that. I guess whatever ghosts Mr. Armbruster saw were calling to him to leave this mortal existence."

In silence, the pair returned to the outer shack that housed all that was the Greater London Investigators of the Paranormal. Tam returned to reading the news off her laptop while Gareth made some tea. Just as the whistle started blowing on the tea kettle, Tam found some recent online articles on supernatural sightings, which gave her pause. They described recent sightings by many Londoners. All of the witnesses agreed that figures were forming from dust and appeared to be menacing them. Nothing bad had happened, but every one of the more recent witnesses said they felt extreme dread, as if their lives were in danger. Checking back on previous articles, past witnesses, when questioned, had not felt this dread. She silently wondered and the questions sprang forth in her mind in quick succession; *what was different from a few days back to now? What will happen if these manifestations gain in strength and frequency? In some way, has the spirit world changed, altered? Are these the 'end days' and this is just the beginning of the Biblical Rapture?*

Gareth brought Tam her tea just as she finished the article. She looked up at him with that winning smile of hers and calmly told Gareth, "We are going to break into Mr. Armbruster's flat tonight."

Chapter Three

Mrs. McIlwraith found herself moved to annoyance by the incessant knocking from the young man and woman that were trying to talk to Mr. Armbruster. *Leave the dead be*, was her final thought on the matter as she closed her window and went to serve High Tea to her husband. Mr. and Mrs. McIlwraith ate their meal; which consisted of beef stew, a round loaf of bread and butter, and tea, while watching some television. Just like Mr. Armbruster, they were also retired and living on a small pension. They had not known the man that had lived next door. They kept to themselves and did not fraternize with the other tenement dwellers. It was not that they felt superior to any of their neighbors; it was due more to the cross-population of the tenement dwellers themselves.

When the McIlwraith's first moved in almost fifteen years ago, there were only pensioners like themselves. A few years back, young couples of gay men and women were moving in, then prostitutes and drug dealers followed. Now there was even a growing gang element of mostly Asian youth moving in. The McIlwraith's did not want to be bothered with these people and their sordid affairs so they kept to themselves. They had a few friends and family that visited from time to time, so they were not wanting for visitors. They did notice though, as the aforementioned types moved in, their frequency of visitors seemed to be dropping. The McIlwraith couple thought of moving, but at their age and fixed income it was almost an impossible idea.

Mr. McIlwraith often fell asleep in front of the evening television and it was up to Mrs. McIlwraith to poke him until he got up and went to bed. She, herself, would often stay up late watching TV. Over the last few nights, while she had been watching the late shows, she had seen ghosts moving about her living room. Two ghosts, she was sure of this. Two ghosts had recently started haunting their flat.

Now, the place seemed to be haunted too.

She was not scared of ghosts as she was Scottish. Growing up, all she heard were ghost stories. This castle was haunted. That lake was haunted. Here is a wedding dress haunted by a jilted bride; the stories were endless. She decided not to mention the ghosts to her husband, as he thought the ideas she learned during her upbringing quite daft. She knew just what he would say.

"Ghosts? Maisie, there're no such things as ghosts! Your parents and brothers told that old lore, to scare you at night, to make sure you stayed good and followed rules. There are bad things out there like serial killers and rapists and terrorists, but there are no ghosts. We need have no fear from the departed. They are in a happier place and would not want to stick around here while they had heaven to get to."

After thirty-five years of marriage, she knew he'd say something like this, if not exactly this. Therefore, for the last week she stayed up and encountered the ghosts. The first few times she saw them, she thought her eyes were playing tricks on her. It seemed like a few bits of dust were blowing around the flat and she didn't think much about it. The last few nights she had been able to make out shapes, as if the dust specks were accumulating and creating a stronger form. Last night, she was certain the ghosts appeared as two young men. Not boys, but lean, muscular men. She wondered if she were having hot flashes, like some of her friends told her they had during menopause. She was long past menopause though and dismissed this idea. *They are not part of my imagination; they are real ghosts.*

With increased interest as to why they were just appearing now, after having lived in the tenement for fifteen years, she stayed up to see if they would appear again. She watched several shows before she noticed the coalescing dust, or ectoplasm, or whatever it was. She rubbed her eyes to make sure she was not too tired and could focus well on the sight. She could hear her husband loudly snoring in the bedroom. Almost one by one, as if in slow motion, dust seemed to appear and move around the room. At first, the dust moved slowly, then after an hour or so it moved faster, swirling into a faint outline in grey. She could make out the silhouette of one young man and then another, standing next to the first. This time, the dust was thicker than in days past and she could almost make out clothes the specters must have worn into death.

Maisie McIlwraith was quickly approaching her eightieth birthday, had already attended many funerals of her family and friends, and did not fear death, but for some reason she could not understand, these specters were making her fearful. They had never done anything, but their increasing definitiveness was perplexing in an unpleasant way. Maisie sat frozen in her easy chair as the images gained in clarity. Maisie could clearly tell that two young men were materializing and the added clarity allowed her to see they were wearing the same type of outfit, like a uniform. Maisie thought of waking her husband to see this manifestation, but a fear she could not place kept her rooted to her chair.

She rubbed her eyes again just to make sure she was really seeing the ghosts. She also took a quick glance at the mantle clock, 12:38AM. She looked back and they still stood between her and the telly. Without reason, she decided to try to talk to them.

"Who or what are ye'? You haff no business wit' an ol' woman like me. Be gone spirits!" Her voice quivered and the sibilant tones of her Scottish accent thickened as she uttered this message.

She saw the ghosts move for the first time. One of them appeared to turn his head to the second one and then turned back to look at Maisie. Then she noticed one of them took a slow step toward her. Whatever it was, it had eyes that seemed to radiate pure black. Her heart was pounding as the thing took one slow step after another. It looked as if it took the spirit a massive effort to move. It came on slow and deliberate as if the legs of the thing weighed a ton. All the while, Maisie stood transfixed by fear and awe. With a twisted fascination, she watched as the dust-ghost-man moved to stand directly in front of her. Then it reached up an arm and swung a ghostly hand at her head. She closed her eyes to await the impact, but the only sensation she had was as if a slightly wet leaf had raked across her cheek.

She opened her eyes and the ghosts were gone.

It was just then that she heard screams and shouting in the next flat over, the newly vacant flat of the recently departed Mr. Armbruster.

Chapter Four

Tam spent the late afternoon putting together two kit bags for her and Gareth. She put in all the equipment they would need to break into the Armbruster flat and conduct a paranormal investigation. With her twisted logic, she reasoned that breaking in was not a crime as they would not take anything. They were actually like detectives and she hoped the reputation of the GLIP would help vouchsafe their deed in the event of police involvement. *There won't be any police called for at that place. The drug dealers alone would never stand for it*, she thought as she finished packing.

Tam carefully hid some skeleton keys, which she managed to buy off a locksmith of ill repute, for a hefty price, inside the lining of her own coat. These had been useful in the past when they conducted investigations at abandoned country estates. She also packed each one of them a large infrared torch light, a 48-LED IR infrared night vision illuminator light for their closed-circuit TVs, a full-spectrum digital camera apiece, mini-monitors and cables, a thermal grid thrower, one thermal camera, an EMF meter to check for electro-magnetic disturbances, and some sandwiches and cold coffee.

She was pleased with her packing job and felt she had everything they would need for a little ghost hunting. Tam and Gareth had gone their separate ways after trying to see Mr. Armbruster. Tam had told Gareth not to meet her at the GLIP headquarters until about 8PM, so she had time to think and research. As she proceeded to turn on her laptop, she thought briefly about Gareth. He always seemed so eager to help in the GLIP operations...*No*, she thought, *it is really for my sake he hangs around so much. What am I going to do with him? He never makes any advances, but I think he has a crush on me. He's always following me around like a puppy dog and tries too hard at being polite to me. I'll just have to be firm with him and make sure he understands paranormal investigations are my calling in life and I don't have time for a boyfriend. He's a good worker and I would hate to lose him, but I can't let him slow me down either.*

Her laptop booted up, and Tam started to search the internet. She decided first to do a search for 'ghost sightings,' but quickly realized that she would have to narrow down her search to get any useful results. So, she added 'news' to the filter and also clicked on 'last week.' She clicked 'Enter' and found herself taken aback by all the recent posts about sightings. Being one of the founders of the GLIP and having an interest in the paranormal all her life, she had often done searches for sightings and a few always popped up from various places around the world, but today was different. Just in the last week, several hundred listings for ghost sightings had gone online, some even from high-end, reputable news services. Almost all of the sightings centered on the London area.

Just as she was reading the tenth or so article, Simon entered. "Hey, Tam, thanks for returning my car so quickly. Got any hot leads for us?" Tam motioned Simon over to where she sat with her laptop. When he came over she pointed at her monitor and said; "Look at all of these recent sightings. Most of these have started popping up on news services and blogs within the last few days and almost all of them are from the London area."

"That's weird. Hey! Are there any new horror films out right now?"

Tam blurted "what?" as she craned her head to look at Simon.

"You know, Tam...Whenever there's a new horror film out, we seem to get more 'sightings.' Usually, they're tied to film publicists trying to whip people into a frenzy to go to the theatre for some shrieks."

Tam turned her head back to the screen. "Simon, look at all of these articles and posts. These are legitimate articles, some even from the bigger news agencies. Something is certainly happening more than just a new horror film coming out. Did you know that we received eleven calls by midday today?"

"Eleven? Now that is a record for us. Are there any paying clients yet?"

Tam scrunched up her face and crossed her arms, as she replied, "No." She thought of how much even a small cooperative like the GLIP cost to run and maintain and it was often a sore subject with her. Whatever funds they did manage to earn, or get donated, were always quickly depleted which caused a constant state of financial unease for her as GLIP President and Chief Accountant. She acquired both positions, as nobody else had wanted those responsibilities. All of the members loved being up all night, using advanced technology, finding wisps, eerie lights and the usual paranormal trappings, but they shunned almost any real responsibilities.

"Buck up, Tam. I'm sure we'll get one soon. Look. We have some unheard messages on the phone." With that, Simon pressed the 'messages' button and a stream of calls issued forth. Some sounded like fakes, which was often the norm, but quite a few sounded serious.

Beep! "Hello. My name is Steve and I'm being haunted. A rather small spirit arises and haunts me all night long. I need the assistance of some of the better-looking female members of your group as this is a bit embarrassing. You see, the spirit arises in my pants and demands to be let out!" Laughing followed and the sound of a phone hanging up.

Beep! "Good evening (hic). My name ith (hic) Ewan and my ex-fucking wife (hic) ith haunting me! She ith not dead...the bitch...but she appears at every bar I'm at and starts yelling at me for money. I'll be (hic) at The Black Horse having a pint after I leave thith pub (hic). Find me there so you can stop the bitch from haunting me!" phone click.

Beep! "Hello. This is the manager of the Roman House Apartments here in London. Normally we would not make a call like this, but many of our renters are complaining about what apparently are ghosts in the buildings. We would be interested in hiring your firm to make an inspection. Please return my call to set up an appointment." The caller left a return number, then the sound of a phone disconnecting.

There were a few more calls, mostly from older people that mentioned ghosts or materializations of some kind within their homes or places of business.

Simon turned back to Tam and said, "Well, well. It certainly looks as if business may be picking up for us after all. That one call from the apartment manager sounded like it might yield some serious scratch for us. I know we can really use that money to keep afloat."

Tam was silent for a moment, thinking over the more serious of the calls. "Yes, absolutely. Can you return that call and assemble a team to check it out, to see if it's legit? Just do a routine set up. I've got something going with Gareth for tonight."

Simon walked behind Tam and placed his hands on her shoulders. He started giving her a massage. "Gareth, huh? You seem to be seeing a lot of him lately." Tam grabbed his hands and made him move to her side where she could see him better.

"Oh Simon, you know he doesn't mean anything to me. We're just colleagues and I've had to spend a lot of time training him. Besides, he's always ready to lend a hand, unlike a lot of you lazy lot." She smiled up at Simon, still holding his hands.

Just then, Gareth walked in.

Tam and Simon turned to look and watched Gareth turn around and walk out while slamming the door behind him. Tam and Simon looked at each other for a second and then back at the door as they heard a knock. Tam dropped Simon's hands and yelled, "Come in!" Gareth came back in with a look on his face that at one moment appeared sheepish, but also a little angry. He mumbled, "Sorry if I'm interrupting something."

Tam had no idea what was wrong with him, but replied easily, "No. You're not interrupting anything. Actually, you and I are all set for tonight. I was just going over some details with Simon. He's going out on another call."

Simon smiled at Gareth and said, "Yes. You and Tam get to work together tonight. I wish I were as lucky. You'll have a great time, I'm sure."

"I could switch with you, if you really want to, and let you go with Tam."

Simon moved toward the door and replied, "No. I have more experience and therefore I'm needed elsewhere tonight. Just learn from Tam and you'll be going on investigations like the rest of us before you know it. Have fun tonight." His hand did a one-arc wave in the air as he stepped out of the shack into the rapidly approaching dusk, shutting the door behind him.

Tam looked at Gareth and saw that he looked unwell. "Gareth, if you're not feeling up to going out tonight, I can get someone else."

"No Tam. I'm fine. I want to go." He just couldn't tell her how much he really wanted her and how much it bothered him to see her so matey with Simon.

Tam went ahead and detailed all of her preparations for tonight; the gear, how the set up would go, even down to the sandwiches and coffee. Since Tam had already loaded up and checked their investigation tools, they put on their packs and decided to walk the two miles to the flats were Mr. Armbruster had lived...and died. They had read Mr. Armbruster's brief obituary in the paper and hoped that his apartment would still be empty as his death was so recent.

As they walked, Tam explained that by walking, it would give them more time for it to get "good and dark", and without a car, it would be harder for the police to tag them after they were finished breaking into Mr. Armbruster's domicile. Besides, the truth was that Tam enjoyed walking for exercise.

The tenement flats were already as dark and quiet as a forgotten tomb when they arrived. No one was hanging around. Most of the exterior lights were out, but many windows had the soft glow of light showing through various window screens and curtains. They quietly made their way up the stairs to the flat in question. Tam rang the door buzzer twice, just to make sure no one was inside. After a full two minutes of waiting, she took out her lock pick tools and quickly popped the door open. It was almost too easy. The door lock was practically an antique.

Tam went in first, tugging on Gareth's shirtsleeve, and pulling him in with her. Once they were inside, she quietly shut the door and both of them were standing in total darkness, the only sound being their breathing. Gareth heard a slight noise as Tam turned on a small LED light on a headband she must have put on after shutting the door. It was like the kind of headlamp a coal miner might have worn, but newer and smaller. Whispering or using hand signals, the two deftly set up all of the equipment to conduct a paranormal investigation. They set up a grid in the main room, where they believed Mr. Armbruster saw his ghost, and then checked that all cameras were on and recording.

Tam signaled that she would watch the cameras on a monitor she had set up. She indicated that she wanted

Gareth to continually check the EMF meter for any fluctuations and record the time and any happenings in a small notebook. Gareth had also been fitted with a headlamp so he could see the notebook in order to write in it. Once all was situated to Tam's desire, she whispered to Gareth what he may expect to see; maybe a faint form walking by or maybe the movement of some item.

As the hours ticked off, nothing happened. Gareth was feeling like a fool. Why did I join this silly group of loonies? I don't even believe in ghosts! I must be hard up, thinking I had to get to know Tam more than any other girl. Shit! She doesn't like me anyway. She obviously likes Simon. Why else would they have been holding hands? Just as Gareth thought he would try to make some small talk with Tam in hopes of seeing if he even had a chance with her, he heard her lightly gasp.

Whispering loudly, Tam said, "Gareth! Do you see that? Check your meter! Get the data!"

Gareth looked at the EMF meter and saw it had spiked. The needle was all the way in the 'red' indicator area. He knew if the meter wasn't broken, something big was happening. He looked around but could only see some dust swirling in the glow emitted from their infrared equipment. He squinted around the room and saw the dust was moving faster and appeared to be gaining definitiveness of form and was gaining speed in movement.

"Tam! What's this? Is this what a ghost looks like? Is this normal?"

"No! I've never seen a manifestation like this before. This is something different. Come over here, quick!"

Gareth moved over to where he could see what was on her monitor. It was much easier to see a shape was materializing on her screen. They both could clearly see it was in the shape of a man. As they watched, transfixed, the form kept gaining definition and movement. At first, the shape had appeared near the back wall of the flat, but it had crossed the floor and had walked halfway to where they were. They could clearly see it was the form of a man in his twenties and he was wearing a uniform of some sort. He was moving closer. Tam and Gareth stood frozen in a mix of fear and awe. They proceeded to watch both the monitors and the actual dim figure as it continued moving toward them. It progressed to materialize and they could see facial features developing. The ghost had a hateful sneer and its eyes were solid black. As it got within a few feet of the two, it raised its right arm and brought it down on top of Tam's monitor. With a small flash, the monitor blew its circuitry and went dead, making the room even darker.

Tam and Gareth both screamed and Gareth yelled, "Run!" as he pulled Tam up and toward the door. The pair ran out of Mr. Armbruster's flat, but promptly tripped over each other and fell on the dimly lit landing, staring into the dark apartment. They hugged each other and waited for something to overtake them as they sat where they had fallen, but nothing happened. They stared into the dark apartment, but saw no movement. Just then, Mrs. McIlwraith called out to them from her opened window, "You two, eh? Whass all tha screaming fer? It should've been me tha was screaming. I chuss got attacked by two ghosts while you two is playin' around!"

Tam and Gareth stared at her in dumbfounded wonderment.

Gareth finally said, "You saw two ghosts?"

"Yes. Funny thing...they both wore those nazi armbands...Swat-tikis, I think they is called."

Chapter Five

London, England
Nine months earlier

Ian Sayer had become a media figure when he led the discovery to the greatest recovery of Nazi gold and the release of his book; *Nazi Gold* in 1984. Sayer was now retired from his many business ventures and spent most of his time evaluating and cataloging his collection of more than 25,000 war documents. Just by sheer accident, Ian found a small document pressed between the pages of a book on the occult once owned by Reichsfuhrer Heinrich Himmler. The small slip of yellowed paper had fallen out of the book he had been cataloging. He picked it off the floor, fascinated by what he read. It was in German, but he was able to read German as easily as he was able to read English, his native language.

Top Secret Communiqué

DESTROY AFTER READING
Date: May 2nd, 1945
To: Reichsfuhrer Himmler
Regarding:

Shadowfall

Unternehmen Schattenschlag
(Operation Shadow Strike)

The final outcome of the operation has been aborted. Due to the dispatch we received earlier, we destroyed all properties and equipment as instructed. All men left behind have been terminated. Schmitt fled through the Unternehmen Werwolf network with Colonel Hartmann. Only my lieutenant and I remain. I am giving us two more hours to complete the obscuring of the base. After that time, we will no longer exist either unless we receive further orders before our deadline.

Death or Glory,

Major Flauber, SS

These particular bits of paper intrigued Ian the most. The Germans said volumes in a paragraph or two. They were masters of being covert and keeping information vague to outsiders. Of course, he knew some of the names. Major Flaubert was an SS major who was reported to have been killed around May 2nd 1945 by a self-inflicted gunshot wound. *I guess his operation, whatever it was, did not turn out for him.* He also knew that Unternehmen Werwolf (Operation Werewolf) was supposed to have been made up of five-thousand men recruited from the Hitler Youth and that they were never proven to have been very successful. These men were supposed to act as guerilla fighters behind Allied lines to cripple their advancement into Germany. In some documents, he had previously discovered that late in the war, high-ranking officers were using the network to help them escape Europe. This very network helped men like Josef Mengele escape to South American countries where they could hide themselves amidst the lax laws and high populations of loosely documented peoples. *It may even be that small vestiges of Operation Werewolf are still helping to conceal aging Nazis even today*; he thought as he pondered what to do with this information.

Ian went to his computer and looked for information on any SS officers named Schmitt and found only one. Walter Schmitt –Obergruppenfuhrer (Lieutenant General) who was twenty-five years old when he joined the Nazis in 1940. Besides this information, the only other material about Schmitt was limited to rank changes between the years 1940 to 1944; when he became an SS officer. There were no family records, no death record, nothing.

Next, Ian searched the internet for any mention of 'Unternehmen Schattenschlag,' but nothing came up. He also checked the index for his own archive and didn't find anything. He realized whatever this operation was; it must have been highly secretive and undocumented. If he could figure out what this secret mission that translated into 'Operation Shadow Strike,' he knew he would have the makings for a great story to write an article or book; depending on what he could uncover about it. He thought about this and decided since he did not have any information on this secret Nazi mission, he would have to check out the archives held elsewhere in Europe.

Ian didn't care too much for the way the Israeli Mossad operated. Their secret service often worked in an underhanded way; breaking laws in other countries, and torturing people for information, in their zeal to hunt down aging Nazis. Even so, he knew he needed access to parts of the Israeli war archive to further some of his own investigations into more hidden Nazi wealth and this newly discovered, and undocumented, operation. The information he held may be a good bargaining chip to gain that access. He decided to call the head of the Mossad, Tamir Pardo, and offer to share this information in exchange for access to their archive.

Diamante Province, Argentina
Three months earlier

An old man has just finished a day working in the vineyard. The aged man no longer picked the grapes himself as he is too old, but was still paid to train and oversee the many younger pickers. The old man has enjoyed living in this sleepy region of Argentina, with its beautiful landscapes and warm coastal waters. The man has lived a good life, a healthy life. Although his wife passed away several years ago, he is not lonely. Several other older men work the vineyards who he has known for decades and enjoys talking, drinking, and fishing with them at every chance. While walking to his home, the elderly man realized just how good life has been for him. He entered his place, cooked a good meal topped with one of the many fine Cabernet Sauvignons of the region, and went to bed not knowing this would be his last time sleeping in his own bed.

Around three in the morning, they came for him.

Tel Aviv, Israel
Today

Walter Smith, having suffered imprisonment and relentless interrogation for the last three months, about his past, is laying on a cot within a small cell at Mossad headquarters. He is thinking about what has happened and what will be. At ninety-nine years of age, Walter does not fear death, but has no interest in going before he has to. Luckily, his years of freedom have clouded the buried memories of his past. Walter has told the Mossad interrogators little even though they try to fatigue him at every interview. Walter senses they know very little about him. After countless sessions, Walter finally admitted that he was Walter Schmitt, Obergruppenfuhrer (Lieutenant General) for a small SS detachment, but he has not admitted to anything else. The truth is Walter does not want to remember anything from his past. Walter has had to live with the nightmare of his participation during the last days of the war and it has taken a lifetime to bury the information in his mind, which the interrogators want.

Walter has learned little from them, but can tell they felt frustrated by their lack of information on him. Walter knows his records were expertly destroyed by the Nazi SS themselves, and that all they have on him is a birth date, name, rank, and his history of living as a picker and foreman in the vineyards of Argentina. They have asked him repeatedly about the project he was to carry out, but they obviously know nothing about it. Walter will not tell them anything or admit to having heard the name of the operation. Walter Smith would rather face his own death than discuss what he had been a party to in the Black Forest of Germany during that final effort to win the war. Just the name, Unternehmen Schattenschlag, which they say in English as Operation Shadow Strike, conjures the dead faces of ten-thousand men before him.

No. He cannot tell them anything about it. Walter will rot in his cell or die at their hands before he tells them. Walter has lived a tough life and his will is strong. The world will never know about his assignment and the great cost of it in lives. The world will never know that he has the blood of ten-thousand men on his hands alone.

During the last three months in this cell, Walter has had no contact with the outside world. He doubts that even his friends or his adopted government of Argentina know what has happened to him. As a former Nazi and member of the elite SS, he figures the Mossad acted quickly and quietly to extract him from Argentina rather than spend years trying to extradite a man that surely will not live long enough to enter a court or tribunal. Walter eats three meals a day; he enjoys a private courtyard for exercise, gets books to read, and, lately, the privilege of receiving a newspaper daily. Walter cannot get a local paper from Argentina, but since he knows English besides Spanish and German, they bring him the London Times. Overall, he is comfortable, but he does dream of the sun and sea and hopes against hope he may yet find a way back to his adopted Argentina.

Today, he read something that both terrified him and yet offered him hope.

He read the article three times before summoning the guards, telling them he wanted to see the head of Mossad immediately. He had to tell them everything he knew before they took a chance and let him out of his cell. Walter carried the folded newspaper with him. They quickly ushered him into the main interrogation room and sat him down. He sat alone for only a few minutes before the regular interrogator came in.

He met the man's eyes and matter-of-factly stated, "I will not talk to you. This is beyond you. I will only divulge the nature of my assignment to your chief, Tamir Pardo." No amount of talking could get another word out of Walter. His mind was a steel trap now, sprung by the article in the English paper. It took nearly two hours before the head of the Mossad finally appeared in the interrogation room. He made everyone leave and he sat face to face with Walter Smith, a.k.a. Nazi SS Obergruppenfuhrer Walter Schmitt. Pardo did not say hello, but sat meeting Walter's stare for a few minutes before saying in highly accented English, "I am here. What do you want to tell me?"

Walter met Pardo's stare with the renewed courage and will, brought about by what he had read in the newspaper sitting on his lap. Although Pardo had been following this case, he had never met Walter before now. Pardo assumed he would face a shattered man, beaten by his isolation and imprisonment. Pardo could tell instantly that this was not the case with the man now before him. He had seen this look before. Pardo had made a study of faces and expressions. This man, Walter, had some cards to play. Walter Smith had some hope of escaping prosecution by the Mossad, the Israeli

Shadowfall

government, or the Wiesenthal Center. In short, Walter had something to trade.

Walter Smith looked at Pardo and smiled. "Do you believe in ghosts Mr. Pardo?"

Chapter Six

London, England
Today - Morning

"Good morning London! This is Amelia Ainsley with the BBC. We are here at the headquarters of the Greater London Investigators of the Paranormal, otherwise known as GLIP. London awakes today after a rash of ghost sightings over the last few nights, most reported to local police and media outlets. My first question for Tam Winthrop, one of the senior members of GLIP, is why so many sightings right now?"

Tam was excited, but also nervous. GLIP had never received this much serious attention before and she wanted to be at her best. She looked directly into the camera as a bead of sweat fell from her forehead, with more sweat coming. Her voice seemed to have a slight crack in it as she spoke.

"Well, there are sightings all the time, of course, but what we are experiencing right now appears to be a paranormal event of seismic proportion." *Did I really just say 'seismic proportion'? I sound like I am quoting from the Ghostbusters films.* "We have just started our investigations and we hope to know more soon, but I can tell you we have never seen anything of this sort before. This seems like a haunting on a massive scale and we are currently at a loss as to explain why it is happening right now."

"Thanks Tam. Please keep us informed on any further developments. Just one more question for now, do you have any advice for people that may witness one of these manifestations?"

"Yes. First, do not be afraid. A ghost is merely a shadowlike manifestation of someone who has departed. That means what you see should not be able to interact with you in any way, except to scare you. If you are worried, you can walk away. Ghosts are bound to certain areas they haunt and cannot follow you."

Amelia moved her handheld mic away from Tam, turned toward the camera, and spoke.

"Great advice from GLIP. Please remember to stay calm above all. Maybe make yourself a nice cup of tea and turn some lights on until the spirit has disappeared." She paused, and then said, "now for the farm report."

The cameraman yelled 'clear' and that was the end of the shoot. The media left the GLIP shack and drove away in the pursuit of other bits of sundry news from the greater London area.

When they were alone again, Gareth spoke to Tam.

"Why did you lie like that?"

"What are you talking about?"

"You know. That bit about the manifestations not being able to interact with the living. You know that is not true. Not after what happened to us and Mrs. McIlwraith last night."

"Look Gareth, we don't know for sure what we're up against yet and far be it from me to be the one to start a panic. As far as we know, manifestations should not be able to touch us in any real way. Sure, maybe they can knock over a dish, or someone may feel a cold sensation passing by them, but getting hurt by one is unheard of."

"I hope you're right. What Mrs. McIlwraith experienced sounded more like a hard physical slap than just a passing 'cold sensation.' Not to mention the destruction of an expensive piece of our equipment, like the monitor, dented as if by a heavy blow. You might look like a fool if things get worse."

"I know, but if things get worse, my little interview won't matter. People will be too scared to remember what I said. We just need to focus on what is really going on here and see if there is any course of action to deflate the situation. Maybe we need to contact some Catholic priests and talk over Rites of Exorcism with them."

Gareth looked at Tam with a stunned expression on his face. Tam had always maintained that she was an agnostic, bordering on atheist, and never put faith in any of the world's religions. He knew Tam must have been feeling pretty lost and bewildered by last night's events if she was talking exorcism. Tam just stared at a spot on the table in front of her, a puzzled look on her face.

Just then, Simon walked in.

"Good morning, my fellow GLIP comrades! How goes it? Did you two have any success with the spook hunt last night? I had an incredible experience I can't wait to share, but you two must tell me about your story first. I saw the TV crews as they left. You two must have something juicy to tell."

Tam turned to Simon and motioned for him to sit down with them at the table. Once Simon sat down, Tam started to talk about what they experienced last night in her matter-of-fact reporting style. Simon knew Tam was extremely serious about paranormal investigation and anything she told him, he would accept as fact. For Tam not to chastise him for using the term 'spook hunt' must mean she was really distracted by something that happened. He listened in rapt awe of what she told him. When she finished, she asked Simon to report.

"Well, what a night! I can tell you it was chock full of manifestations. Of course your night sounded thrilling, but you will never believe it when I tell you I got information on twenty different apparitions!"

Tam and Gareth dropped their jaws in unison and awaited Simon's tale.

"So, I rounded up Heidi, Astrid, and David and the four of us, made it out to the Roman House Apartments. We must have made quite a spectacle to the sleepy residents there, with our GLIP uniforms and electronic equipment. Anyway, we met the manager, who asked us to be as discreet as possible. Ha! He had no idea what a full investigation entails in equipment set-up and monitoring. We took over the whole works and just as we had settled in to await the happenings, we heard residents screaming from within their various apartments. Having enlisted the manager to answer resident calls and dispatch us to rooms, we spent half the night running from room to room answering distress calls.

The first call we answered was in apartment 14b. An elderly couple rented this apartment. When we arrived, we actually caught our first glimpse of the ghosts. They had been slowly chasing the couple around their rooms and had knocked over several vases and such, but when we got to 14b, we found the tenants huddled together just outside their closed apartment door. We could hear knocking sounds coming from the other side of their door - from inside!

We made the couple move far down the hall and then I opened the door and saw two ghosts in what appeared to be Nazi uniforms! They were not like the ghosts we typically see, you know, the wispy white smoke variety. These two blighters seemed to be made of swirling dust that gave them their substance. Well, these two things started to move slowly toward me with their black eyes ablaze, but dissolved with their first steps and were gone."

Simon went on to describe further encounters and claimed that Astrid even felt a light punch to her midsection from one of the apparitions. The GLIP team had experienced twenty different ghosts, all of them in pairs, having a similar appearance, and seemingly bent on the destruction of the tenants.

"The only trouble I had last night was when all the excitement died down and the hauntings were over, the manager did not want to pay the bill I gave him. In the end, he decided to pay us the five-hundred pound notes to safeguard himself. He decided he better be our client with some say in how we handle things, rather than not pay us and give us room to tell our story to the press and give the Roman House Apartments bad publicity. I must admit I felt rather like a blackmailer when I convinced him to see this point."

Tam felt stunned by everything Simon said. Simon and Gareth were both still new to paranormal investigation and they lacked her deep knowledge she had gained over a lifetime of reading everything she could on such matters. She knew there had never ever been a haunting of this scale before and she felt rattled by it. She had to make some sense of it all and she decided the three of them should go over what they know.

In the end, they made a bullet list on a wipe board that hung on the wall. It read:

- Male apparitions, young, black eyes –no pupils
- Usually in pairs, but sometimes alone
- All wearing same uniform: World War II Nazi
- Coalesced from dust
- Move slowly
- Could interact lightly with items/people
- Short duration of haunt

The three looked over the list and pondered what the situation was. Simon had given Tam a light shoulder rub as she sat and thought up what she should put on the list. Gareth had written the list with her recommendations. Gareth wished that he could be the one to give Tam massages and was finding himself quite angry with Simon. He knew why. He was not stupid. He knew he wanted to date Tam, but had no idea how to get her attention.

"Gareth, we're going back to the apartments again tonight to see what else develops. Perhaps you would like to go with my team?" spoke Simon.

Gareth turned to face Simon and with a tone of bitterness said, "I bet you'd like it if I went in your place so you could have Tam all to yourself tonight."

Shadowfall

Tam spoke next. "What are you talking about? You got it all wrong. Simon wants you to go with *him* and his team."

"I'll bet he just wants to keep an eye on me," said Gareth, as he threw down the wipe-board marker and stormed out of the GLIP shack, slamming the door behind him. Not knowing where to go, he sat in the backyard on a little bench near some rose bushes.

A few minutes of his brooding went by before Tam finally came out and sat next to him. They sat in silence for a moment before she told him, "Look Gareth. I'm not sure what is going on here, but you hurt Simon's feelings and that is bad for team members to do to each other. What is going on with you two anyway?"

Gareth turned to face Tam. In the afternoon sunlight, her golden tresses seemed to glow and the light reflected in her eyes in a way that was simply intoxicating to Gareth. Losing himself, he spoke the truth and gave himself away to her.

"I think I like you Tam. At least I want to date you and see what could develop between us. I want to spend all of my time with you, but I wonder if I even have a chance. Simon obviously likes you too and maybe you prefer him. I'll leave you alone if you like Simon. Just tell me Tam...Do I have a chance with you?"

Chapter Seven

Tel Aviv, Israel
Today – Afternoon

Tamir Pardo, the head of the Israeli intelligence agency known as the Mossad, could not believe his ears when asked whether he believed in ghosts. Pardo let out a sound like 'hmmphf' and replied, "No. Why?"

"Mr. Pardo, have you seen the article in today's London Times?"

"No."

Walter took the paper from his lap and lightly tossed it across the table. It landed just in front of Tamir Pardo.

Walter said, "Look at the article on the first page near the bottom. The one with 'Nazi Ghosts' in part of the title..."

Pardo took his eyes away from Walter's and looked at the paper in front of him. From reading the dossier on Walter, he knew Walter had full faculties and his mind was still sharp for such an elderly man. This could not be a trick. He decided there must be something of value to learn from this aged Nazi. Pardo picked it up and found the article. Pardo read it carefully and then put it back down. Meeting Walter's eyes once again, he said, "Okay. So what? Ghost sightings in London and the locals say they appear to be wearing German uniforms and they have what look like swastikas on them. Tell me about it. Where do you fit in with that?"

"I helped to create those ghosts, only they are not really ghosts. The British are under attack from Nazi soldiers. I put this attack into place during the spring of 1945. I will tell you all I know in exchange for allowing me to live out the rest of my days in peace. I know this will all be difficult for you to accept, but there it is."

Pardo did not barter with ex-Nazis, but he also knew that after three months of grilling Walter they had no evidence he had anything to do with the Nazi extermination of the Jews. Members of the SS, all well documented for fanaticism and brutality, however, Pardo had hoped Walter might furnish more information regarding the number of Jews killed, or at least information that might lead to reclaiming hidden Jewish wealth seized by the Nazis.

"Walter, I do not make deals with Nazis, especially SS men. Tell me your story and I may act with leniency toward your case."

"Mr. Pardo, I am so old that Death is almost my friend. Whatever you do to me matters little. I have no family left to grieve for me and I have nothing to lose except for my last few breaths of freedom. I wish to end my days drinking wine, catching fish, and walking the beach at sunrise and sunset while smelling the sweet air of my beloved Argentina. I can tell you what that article alludes to, is only the beginning of what will be a reckoning that will end in the deaths of thousands, perhaps even hundreds of thousands of British citizens. I have lived with the death of ten thousand men on my head for decades. I don't want to add any more lives to that count, but if you do not grant my freedom, I will have no choice."

"If you killed ten thousand men, I will not be able to grant you anything other than a life sentence, or execution. We hunt your kind for redemption of our people. You may call it revenge, but nonetheless, we are the only judge and jury left to work for the silent voices of the six million Jews you Nazis killed in cold blood. If you are reluctant to divulge the whole nature of your assignment, then let us start with the men you killed. Can you discuss that? How does that figure in with your secret assignment, and are the deaths related to it? You must give me something to work with, something to help me make determinations."

Walter quietly thought for a few seconds and then launched into his story, "I was only twenty-five years old when I first enlisted in the army. My mother had been an occultist during the 1920s and 1930s. I grew up in a home that welcomed the supernatural, and my home boasted strange and fantastic curios. My mother had an amazing library that held many books on mysticism and the occult. I grew up reading all of these books and often helped my mother. She was a medium of the first order. Some even said her skills were too good; she must have used witchcraft. Historically, we persecuted witches during all ages of Germany's past, so she downplayed her skills as much as possible. I honestly do not believe my mother was a witch. I never saw her practice witchcraft. I saw, and even helped, her conduct many séances. She could contact the dead and she possessed a keen sense of déjà vu, but that was the extent of her power; besides the knowledge she had gained from reading her books. No matter, her abilities were strong enough that she had quite a reputation and her name even reached Heinrich Himmler, who you know was the head of the Nazi SS and reported directly to Adolf Hitler.

The Nazi party and the army invited me to join. Being a young man without much direction, I blindly joined and found that I quickly moved up through the ranks. I did not realize it at first, but Himmler was watching and grooming me from a distance. He discovered that I also possessed some of my mother's abilities and asked me to join the SS, where I proceeded to rise further in rank. My knowledge of spirits and things of a supernatural nature made me an expert in Himmler's eyes. When Hitler had found the Spear of Destiny...Yes Mr. Pardo, it does exist. The very spear that was stabbed into Jesus while he was crucified...Although you are Jewish, Mr. Pardo, it was this very spear that is mentioned in the Gospel of John and the Gospel of Nicodemus, in the Bible, which a Roman centurion had pierced Jesus with as he was dying on the cross. So, Hitler had the spear and I was called in to authenticate it. I did so and found it to be the legitimate item in question. Hitler and Himmler were both as thrilled as little schoolchildren. I suddenly found myself promoted to Lieutenant General. Hitler tried many things with the spear, but he never really came close to unlocking its potential; at least not until he gave it to me. You see, I needed the Spear of Destiny to aid me with what you call in English, Operation Shadow Strike.

Without giving away the details of my mission, I will tell you about the ten thousand men, whose deaths are on my head. Himmler himself had attached the requisite soldiers to Operation Shadow Strike. They all signed on of their own free will, but what happened to them is the private hell I have kept secret for all of these decades.

I will say no more unless we can agree to my freedom. If you don't free me, the deaths of thousands will also be on your head as well as my own. These events in the paper are only the very beginning. I don't know why there was such a delay, but death is fast approaching now. Only with my help will you save thousands, perhaps even millions, of innocent lives."

Pardo ingested all of this information. He wasn't sure if this man was telling the truth or not, but he would humor him for now and investigate his claims. He asked Walter to give him some names to check the veracity of his story in the archives. Walter gave him the names of officers attached to him and the full name of his mother. Walter returned to his cell. Pardo promised to investigate and get back to him. What he didn't tell Walter was he thought nothing about the London ghost sightings, but at least he had gotten something out of Walter. He would check up on the names Walter mentioned, but at his leisure. Walter was not going anywhere and he was in no rush to make any deals with a Nazi. Besides, Tamir Pardo did not believe in the supernatural.

Chapter Eight

London, England
Today – Late Afternoon

Gareth was packing his equipment for tonight. In a couple more hours, he would be joining Simon and his team to unravel the supernatural events going on at the Roman House Apartments. He remained stunned by the answer Tam had given him to his question regarding whether or not he had any kind of a chance with her. She squinted her eyes at him and mumbled something that sounded like "Men...," clenched her fists and stormed back into GLIP headquarters. *So, does that mean I might have a chance or not? At least she didn't shoot me down completely. I guess I'll just have to wait and see.*

He finished packing and headed to Simon's flat. Just as he was about to knock, Simon opened the door and smiled a second at Gareth before saying, "I saw you coming up the walk. I'm so glad you are joining my team this evening. Come inside and we'll work out our attack plan for tonight." Gareth, still not sure whether to trust Simon or not –at least when it came to Tam, walked in and saw that the front room was empty.

"Am I the first to arrive?"

"Yes. I told you to come at five PM, but the other members won't be here until 5:30PM. I thought this would give us some time to chat. Please have a seat."

Gareth took a seat on the couch nearest the door. "It's time to chat about what?"

Simon leaned against a wall near where Gareth sat. "Well...About your place in the GLIP organization of course...Okay...I really just wanted a chance for us to talk. I thought it would be good if we got to know each other."

Gareth felt uneasy. He did not want to share his feelings for Tam with Simon. As far as he knew, Simon was his only real competition for Tam. *Maybe I'd better leave...*

"Gareth, don't look at the door like you want to leave. I just thought it would be good if we talked a little so we can work well together tonight."

"Okay. What should we talk about?"

"Well...Where did you grow up? When did you get interested in ghosts...the supernatural?"

"I grew up here in Central London. My Dad was a banker —now deceased, and my Mum is a retired schoolteacher. I know its lame, but I still live with her—poor me, right? Well, my Dad died while I was just reaching the secondary education level. I was eleven and it devastated me. My Dad was a great bloke and he spent lots of time with me, at least as much as he could. One day he went to work and never came back. We found out his usual parking space was unavailable that morning, so he parked across the street from the bank entrance and ended up run over by a drunken lorry driver. For a few years after that, I started having conversations with my dad, every night, just before I fell asleep in my bed. I actually believed his ghost was coming every night to give me advice."

"I'm sorry to hear about your dad." Simon leaned forward and gave Gareth a light pat on the arm. "Did your mum think you were going balmy?"

"Sure, but as soon as she found out, he quit coming. He told me he would see me again some day...when it was my time. Of course, I know now this was all just a child's fantasy. I'm not a nutter. He was like an imaginary friend that I grew out of, but it still started an interest within me to seek a way to communicate with the dead, or even discover whether or not ghosts are even real."

Simon shifted legs and maintained leaning against the wall. "So how did you find out about GLIP?"

Gareth hoped he was not turning red in front of Simon. The truth was he had found the organization while doing web searches on ghosts and had been so smitten with the pictures of the beautiful female ghost hunter named Tam that he knew he had to join to get near her. Ever since he first laid eyes on her, he sensed in her someone that would understand his experience with his father and would help him to find answers –together. He thought quickly for an answer to Simon's question and finally blurted out a silly, but partially true, answer.

"Ghosts are fun. I liked Scooby Doo growing up and all the ghost movies I saw just made me even more curious. I found GLIP doing a web search on ghosts."

Just as Gareth was feeling totally humiliated with his answer, Simon's attention was diverted by the doorbell. The other members of tonight's team where here. *Yes!*

Saved by the cavalry! This is what Gareth was thinking as he stood to welcome the newcomers with Simon.

***

The GLIP van had pulled up to the Roman House Apartments and all of the equipment quickly dispersed to the team members to carry into the building. Once in the main lobby, the night manager met the team. The apartment manager informed them to please to be as discreet as possible and not to upset the guests. The manager indicated he knew this was all very out of the ordinary, but also felt it might be necessary. The manager seemed to lack confidence and was at odds with his own decision about allowing GLIP to investigate. Simon helped to calm his fears and promised they would all act with as much decorum as possible. Gareth could not help feeling this all looked like a scene from the film Ghostbusters, but he kept his thoughts to himself.

Altogether, there were six team members on this investigation. Besides Simon and Gareth, there were Billy and Tommy who were twins, and Sally and Blake who were an 'item.' Although the apartments took up fourteen floors, the team decided to stay in groups of two at certain floors. Sally and Blake were to remain in a corner of the lobby with all the monitoring equipment. They would also receive some assistance from the manager who would field disturbance calls. Billy and Tommy went to the fifth floor - main hall. Simon suggested to Gareth that they take the thirteenth floor. "Just for a lark, you know. What with thirteen being unlucky and all, wot say you?" Gareth agreed and all the members moved to their stations, lugging whatever equipment they would need for the night ahead.

It was still light outside when Simon and Gareth reached the thirteenth floor, but they could tell twilight was fast approaching and that meant nightfall right behind it. They staked out an area at the end of the main hall, just under a large stain glass window of roses. They deftly set up all of the electronic apparatus and cameras until all they had left to do was just sit and wait.

"Simon?"

"Yes?"

"Around what time did everything happen last time?"

"Well, no one reported anything big happening until about ten. For some reason, right around ten o'clock is when all hell seems to break loose around here."

Gareth made a mental note that also seemed to fit approximately, time wise, with what he had witnessed. Simon took out his radio and checked in with the others. Everyone was stationed and patiently waiting. Sally and Blake said the monitors were on and working fine. They could see what was happening on the fifth and thirteenth floors with no problem.

Twilight came and quickly gave way to the blanket of night. All of the team members were anxious and ready to see supernatural vague forms of dust and scared inhabitants. The manager had asked the apartment dwellers to stay in tonight and not venture in the halls if they could help it. Because of the previous incident, most either complied or sought lodgings elsewhere for the night. Simon and Gareth sat quietly at their end of the hallway and sipped coffee from a thermos. The hours seemed to drag by. Gareth's thoughts kept going back to

Tam. *Will I ever get anywhere with her?* This thought kept repeating in his mind and distracted him from the passage of time.

Just as all of the GLIP team was starting to get a little tired from being 'at the ready,' it started. The first disturbance began with the screams of an elderly woman. Simon and Gareth ran down the hall toward the room where the screams were coming from, but as they ran, more screams blasted from behind most doors.

Simon and Gareth froze in fear in the middle of the hall and could only listen without knowing how to act. All around them, they could hear pounding on walls, doors, and screams that were unending. The pounding was getting so intense that pictures were falling from the walls and holes were starting to appear in some walls. Gareth stared at a door near him as the door handle rattled and he could hear what sounded like an old man pounding from behind it. He heard muffled prayers between the screaming that blended into one exaggerated sentence. "Please...oh God! Help me! Owww...I can't get out...He's coming! Aaarrrgghh! ...No...You're wrecking everything...I thought you were all dead...He's...choking...me...." Both of them also heard the screams coming from their team members over their radios.

Finally, the door Gareth was staring at opened and an old man stared directly at Gareth for a split second before falling dead to the floor. Blood was flowing rapidly from the man's head. Behind the man, Gareth saw a vague form move in the shadows beyond. It advanced out into the hallway and as it did, the lights in the hall began to blink and dim at the same time, as if the power were about to go out. Gareth tried adjusting his eyes. He blinked several times to clear his vision as sweat was dripping from his brow into his eyes. The figure appeared out of focus. It came on, a misty looking being wearing a uniform that bore a swastika armband on the left arm. Gareth saw the swastika appeared to glow in a spectral green cast while the eyes of the form...the eyes were pure black. They looked dusty, but black. No pupil, no white, all black.

"Run!"

Gareth barely heard the command from Simon, but he reacted just in time to miss an ugly cut by the swing of a kitchen knife from the dust being. Gareth and Simon ran back down the hall toward their equipment. As they did, many doors were now opening and bloody men and women were shuffling or running as best as they could toward the stairs or elevator. Loosely formed men of dust were pursuing them, many carrying physical objects which the beings used as blunt instruments.

The hallway was becoming covered in blood and mayhem. They watched in shock as one old woman was being beaten severely with an alarm clock. Another old man had his face pounded beyond semblance by a cast iron bookend. A yapping dog was bludgeoned to death with the bottom of a floor lamp. The dust beings were intent on killing the apartment dwellers that they had followed out of their respective domiciles and were not paying any attention to Gareth and Simon who had ran back to their camp at the far end of the hall.

The two hid behind their equipment, but as they stole glances, they witnessed the inhabitants of the thirteenth floor under attack.

"Oh shit...Oh shit...Oh shit!" was all that Gareth managed to stammer.

Simon grabbed him and drew him close and shouted, "Gareth, get yourself together!" Just as he said this, a dust man took notice of the pair and ran toward them raising a broken table leg over his head. Simon pushed Gareth away with force and caused the dust man to bring the table leg down on the equipment behind them. The electronics sputtered, sparked, and died. The dust man fell upon the equipment, but did not get up. He lifted his head and looked at Gareth and Simon with a look of pure malevolence emanating from his two pitch black orbs and a hearty smile on his vague face and loudly uttered; "Werden wir sie bekommen!" His sentence trailed off at the end and seemed to echo in the hall as the form began to dissolve and was gone. Gareth and Simon looked down the hall and prepared for more violence, but all of the dust men were swirling away into nothingness.

After a full minute of being incapable to move due to shock, Gareth and Simon helped each other to stand and, together, they inspected the damage. Most of the elderly occupants that made it into the hall were injured, but only two were dead. A few lucky ones were unscathed, but clearly rattled to the point of nervous breakdown. There were holes in walls, broken doors, bits of broken furniture, and of course, some blood. In the distance, they could hear the wail of sirens.

Gareth looked at Simon and spoke; "Hey, thanks back there for pushing me out of the way." Simon turned away from the carnage and met Gareth's look.

"I couldn't let you get hurt. I hope you would've done the same for me. We can talk later. Let's see if we can help any of these people." With that, both of them started combing through the injured to see whom they could comfort or assist.

***

The next morning the London papers were all full of the same story of Nazi ghosts, surprise attack, and death. In the wee hours of the morning, a haggard GLIP team made it back to headquarters, deposited their equipment, and made their separate ways to their various homes. They were glad to find no reporters milling about. They had all heard the various messages from the radio cautioning people and updating happenings around London. It seemed last night's attack was not restricted to the Roman House Apartments.

Just as Gareth was about to turn and leave, Simon grabbed his arm and said, "Look, I want you to know you did fine last night. None of us was ready for that. There was no cowardice in our running or hiding. That event was beyond our capabilities for response. You did very well Gareth as a part of our team and helped those people alongside us when the invasion ended. I guess I just want you to know that I am proud to have you on our team."

Gareth, taken aback by the compliment from his rival for Tam's affections, but was happy that at least he had Simon's respect.

"Thanks Simon."

"Look, Gareth...Why don't you crash here. You can sleep on my couch."

Respect or not, they were still rivals and Gareth could not get that thought out of his mind.

"No thanks, Simon. My mum is probably worried enough as it is."

With that, they said their goodbyes and Gareth went home. The team members swore to meet for lunch to discuss and report last night's occurrence.

Chapter Nine

*Tel Aviv, Israel
Today – early morning*

Tamir Pardo was apprised of situations around the world on a daily basis, but he read with some fascination the events centered on London, England. He read the many accounts of ghost sightings and took special note of their descriptions. There were several different articles that all amounted to about the same information. He just finished reading an atypical news story about the hauntings:

Nazi Terror in London?

Associated Press – London

Last night Londoners claimed attacks in their residences by apparitions. It is too early for an adequate explanation regarding the events, but eyewitness statements agree that the attackers appeared to be ghosts dressed in uniforms with Nazi swastika armbands. Areas around London report differing amounts of damage. Local authorities say upwards of a thousand people reported attacks, while at least two dozen people died from them last night.

Local authorities are rounding up known Neo-Nazi groups for interrogation. A small group of paranormal investigators known collectively as the Greater London Investigators of the Paranormal is also under examination.

Sergeant Bowen told the Associated Press that at this time authorities have no other news to offer except to stay tuned to local radio and the BBC News for any further developments. Bowen also stated the attacks appear to happen at night and warned people to be extra vigilant during the evening hours for anything out of the ordinary.

Local authorities were overwhelmed with calls for assistance last night and there is a rumor of military involvement to assist with keeping the peace tonight in downtown London and suburbs.

***

Pardo put the paper down and thought for a while. It was all too fantastic to believe. Did this 'Smith' character...this Nazi...have the key to what was happening? Pardo had his staff check with London regarding the accuracy of the newspaper reports. His staff reported in the affirmative. The London police were dumbfounded about what was happening and apparently, they were already making calls themselves to the German government and any other authorities on Nazis they could.

Pardo himself made a quick call to Scotland Yard and satisfied himself about the validity of the stories he was reading. His mind was heavy with thoughts about whether he should offer any help or not. He reasoned that if people were dying today, Smith does hold a bargaining chip. Of course, he will not let him escape Mossad justice, but he might be able to use him to help end whatever was happening. He decided to call for Smith.

Smith, extracted from his cell, returned to the same interrogation room as before. Tamir Pardo was already seated and smoking a cigarette. Smith sat across from Pardo and the two men stared at each other, sizing each other up, for a few minutes before Pardo spoke.

"When last we spoke, you mentioned thousands might soon die. Have you read today's English papers?"

"Yes."

"Those stories...ghosts, or whatever...Is that what you were talking about?"

"Yes, but..."

"What?"

"This is just the beginning. Tonight many more will die. Not just dozens like last night, but possibly thousands. Each night the death count will rise until all Londoners are dead."

Pardo looked away from Smith. He took a long drag on his cigarette and stood up. He turned toward Smith and his frustration on how to proceed with his prisoner was evident in his sarcasm. "I suppose this is just what you call good German engineering?"

Smith looked up at Pardo, and, with all of the sincerity that he could produce, said; "Mr. Pardo, we were still at war in 1944. We created a weapon that we hoped would work. Was it 'good engineering,' I would say 'No.' It was supposed to work in 1944, not today...not now."

"Look Smith. All I want is for you to tell me what you did and tell me how I can stop it. Can you do that?"

"No."

Pardo gave Smith a sly look and a smile spread across his face that looked sinister in the harsh lighting.

"I could have you tortured, you know."

"Mr. Pardo. I am old. You would probably kill me before you got anything of any use out of me. I told you before I was on friendly terms with death. With everything I have seen and done in my nine decades, you hold nothing that I fear."

"What about your freedom? Your precious Argentina that you want to return to?"

"I don't have long for this world. If I never see my adopted homeland again, at least I still have my memories."

"Why won't you tell me how to stop all of this? You know you are no longer at war with anyone. You, yourself are surprised by all of this...Why not stop whatever this is and help save innocent lives...The lives of people that don't even remember your war!"

"It is not that I will not tell you. I can't tell you. To be honest, I would need to see what remains before I could figure out how to stop what is now in motion. I have to figure out why it took so long to work before I can figure out how to reverse, or stop, the process."

"Would you be willing to work for your freedom? I mean, if you stop this 'process' and save thousands of lives, would you do that for a ticket back to Argentina?"

"And all actions against me stopped?"

"Yes. You are old without much time left. We could easily forget you." Pardo hoped he sounded truthful, but deep inside he knew this man could never escape his justice. The souls of six million dead Jews depended on him.

Shadowfall

***

They struck a deal. After some negotiation, and the arrangement of some diplomatic papers that would give Walter Smith a temporary visa and diplomatic immunity, they outfitted him with some comfortable clothing, boots, and jacket. Smith met the two men that would accompany him; Levi and Deron, dressed in plainclothes but armed. They looked like the typical type of bodyguards that you saw in movies, Walter thought, dressed in similar suits, ties, rugged leather shoes, and sunglasses. They each had a small backpack slung over their shoulders, which Walter later found out carried a change of clothes similar to that in which they had outfitted him.

Tamir Pardo watched from the tarmac as the plane carrying Walter Smith left Israeli ground, bound for Germany. He knew he would see Smith again, and soon.

German officials had no information about the mission. The fewer people that knew the better, was what Pardo figured. Besides, he didn't want the public to hamper the mission with protests or demonstrations or sympathizers, or whatever else. If this worked at all, it should be done and over with soon. If this did not work, Smith would be back in his cell within a couple of days at the maximum. The harder part was still ahead though. Pardo would have to get the British to cooperate. Somehow, he had to get some experts to oversee Smith. He remembered reading about the Greater London Investigators of the Paranormal. *Yes. They must be experts in dealing with the supernatural.* He would get them to assist Smith in Germany.

Chapter Ten

London, England
Today – midday

As planned, Simon's team met at GLIP headquarters for a light lunch, and to report on their findings at the Roman House Apartments. Tam had gotten up early and made some sandwiches, lemon squash, and tea for the incoming team. She had help in getting up early from reporters pounding on her door demanding a story. She told them all to 'Rack off' as she had no new information to share.

By noon, the members had managed to drag themselves in and have a seat in chairs arranged around the main table. Tam served each one as they came in, all obviously shaken badly. Their eyes were bloodshot from little, or fitful sleep. Some members seemed to shake a little as if chilled and a few others just stared vacantly at their teacup without saying a word. Most members were eager to tell Tam what happened the previous evening, but she shushed them all and told them to wait until Simon got there so they could get all the facts recorded at once.

The GLIP members were all eating quietly in their various states of mind as Gareth walked in. Tam pointed him to a chair and brought him some food. Tam had a big smile and a knowing look as she poured some lemon squash into his cup and asked, "So, how did it go with you and Simon last night?"

"It was terrifying. So we got there and set up and..."

"No! Don't tell me about the events yet. Wait until it is time to make the official report. What I meant was how did you and Simon get on?"

"Oh...Simon is okay. I prefer working with you, but he's a good bloke. We worked together just fine last night." *I would have preferred to be with you, Tam. I joined GLIP in the hope that we could get to know each other and go out on a date. I would like you to forget Simon and be my girlfriend.*

Tam was just about to say something else when in walked Simon. She quickly turned and went to get more sandwiches. Simon made his 'Hellos' and sat down before his formal speech began.

"All right, we had ourselves quite an evening last night and we are here to make a formal report and share our findings. I hope that everyone has had a bite to eat. Okay, let us began. Tam, do you have the recorder?"

Tam went to a corner of the room and returned with a digital audio recorder. She handed it to Simon and he turned it on, checked the recording levels, and began.

"Last night at approximately 1800 hours, the GLIP team entered the Roman House Apartments and..." What followed was a detailed description of the night's events. Everyone contributed what he or she saw, heard, felt, and did...even Gareth. They shared all facts, even the embarrassing ones, but no one criticized the actions of anyone else. Some of the testimonials kept to the facts, while others gave horrific and graphic details while sobbing. In addition, for the record, the group figured out what the ghost had said to Simon and Gareth, using an internet translation program, and typing in the German words as best as they could. They got back 'We will get you,' as the result.

Simon started the new topic. "Okay, we just went over all the events of last night, but what about tonight and every night from here out? It seems whatever is going on is escalating and no one seems to know what to do about it. Let's hear your thoughts, everyone?" The GLIP members theorized for a while, but no one had anything tangible to offer in the way of a key toward stopping the events. Several members stated last night was their final GLIP activity as they were quitting. Around the table, the sentiment was unanimous as most members vocalized that GLIP were not equipped to handle a manifestation of the scale they witnessed last night. There was some argument, some persuasion to stay, but at the end of the meeting, GLIP had lost half its membership.

After the meeting, the members seemed to melt away instead of the typical hanging out. Soon, only Simon, Gareth, and Tam remained. It took two hours to record every detail and theorize about what to do next and everyone felt spent. Tam realized Gareth and Simon needed a lift so she decided it was late enough to get out a few beers and pass them around. Gareth and Simon eagerly took theirs and all of them sat in silence until they heard a loud knocking.

"Come in!" yelled Tam.

The door opened and two men dressed in suits, ties, and sunglasses walked in. They looked like rejects from a spy movie. At least that is what Tam thought about them.

Tam was slightly stunned, but was about to ask them what they wanted when one of them asked first.

"We understand this is the headquarters of the Greater London Investigators of the Paranormal. Is that correct?"

Tam was quick to reply, "Yes. My name is Tam. These two are Simon and Gareth. We are all members of the GLIP...as we call it." Tam thought these two might be foreign reporters after leads regarding last evening's spectral appearances. The man who spoke to her clearly had what sounded like a middle-eastern accent, but she could not quite place it.

The two suited men nodded in unison and said; "We are here on a delicate matter. Of course, you have been following the recent sightings of ghosts in England. We are seeking a few members of the Greater...the GLIP, to come with us and try and stop the cause of these sightings at their source."

Tam and Simon started throwing out many questions in tandem as Gareth sat silently watching the interplay between the two factions. Finally, the suit that had been quiet spoke up.

"Listen. We cannot tell you anything right now. It is not that we don't want to, but we really are not sure what we are facing. We have operatives that are already on the move to what they believe the source of the outbreak is. All we ask is for a few of your best members to go, look, and try to help if possible, all expenses paid, and we will give your organization a donation for your time. Can you elect a few members that can be of help?"

Shadowfall

Tam looked at Simon. Simon looked at Tam. Tam told the men; "We, us two, can go. We are the senior members and the have the most knowledge."

"That is fine. Do you-"

Gareth, who was feeling a little jealous that Tam and Simon would be together, interrupted the man. "Hey! How about me? I know I don't have that much experience, but you will need someone to help you carry all the equipment."

Tam and Simon nodded at each other and asked the suits if that would be all right with them if they took a third member.

"Sure. You can bring him, but we need to leave immediately. We can give you half an hour to pack whatever gear you need. Our car waits out front." The suited men walked out and left the three.

Tam, Simon, and Gareth discussed whether this was a good idea or not. They realized the men had not even shown any credentials. They had no idea who they were or where they came from. They decided that either they were from the government or they were crackpots. Gareth agreed to do whatever Tam and Simon agreed on. Tam and Simon decided no matter whom they were, time was of the essence. The nightly visitations were getting more violent every night. They theorized that if this led them anywhere nearer a solution about what was happening; it would be worth the risk.

The three packed all of their gear and left directives for the other GLIP members. Gareth had to call his mother and let her know that he would be away for a few days and not to worry about him. She related that she was seeing strange things in her home and Gareth made her promise to go and stay with her sister in the countryside for a few days. He told her he loved her and hung up and joined Tam and Simon. Together they headed out front to the waiting car and to whatever they might find at the end of their journey.

Chapter Eleven

Germany

It was nearing five o'clock in the early evening as Walter Smith sat between his Israeli guards, Levi and Deron, at the airport bar drinking a glass of wine. Walter thought about what he could do to stop the 'ghost invasion' as it seemed to be occurring. He ran over all he could remember; all facts, details, anything that might be of use. It was so long ago. Would he even be able to find the right location? Would he really be able to stop what was now in motion after all of these years? He was lost in thought when the experts arrived.

Walter was moved from his reverie by the introductions. He was shocked to see that instead of lab-coat toting scientists, that these were young people! *What would people so young know about these matters? How could they be of any assistance?* He shook hands with the two boys and the girl and they all sat down for a drink. The two Mossad operatives who brought the three young people left. Only Levi and Deron remained. It was the one named Levi that suggested that they all remain quiet and not discuss their 'mission' until they got to their hotel. Everyone finished their drinks and got into a mini-van. It whisked them from the airport to their hotel.

Everything had been prearranged and Levi and Deron led them all directly to a connecting suite with four rooms, each person assigned a room, and encouraged to quickly put their stuff down, use the facilities as needed, and return in ten minutes to a large table in the main room. Once seated, Levi spoke first.

"I think it would be best if we made some introductions, but first let me clear the air of a few questions I assume you have. First…Yes, you are in Germany. You are here on temporary diplomatic visas sponsored by the Israeli government. While here, we will enjoy some diplomatic immunity, but do not take that as an excuse to cause any trouble. My partner and I represent your sponsors here and if there is any trouble, you will answer to our government or us. Second, you are not to discuss our aims with anyone outside of this group. If anyone asks you anything, please allow my partner or me to respond for you. Third, once we are satisfied that the mission is complete, or that you at least have done all that you can, we will send you home. This is with the exception of Mr. Smith. Your outcome is still to be determined. Now, let us make introductions and then perhaps Mr. Smith can explain to the group why we are all here. I will start. You may call me Levi. I am one of your escorts and a member of the Israeli Mossad. My job is to get you where you need to be and back out again, as safely as possible."

Levi motioned to his partner who took up from where Levi left off.

Deron said, "And I am your other escort with the same goals as Levi. My name is Deron and I am also a member of the Mossad." That was all. It was obvious to the group

Shadowfall

Levi was the talkative one and Deron was the silent, stoic one. Levi was used to Deron. He knew that Deron would prefer to stay silent and would only agree with, or repeat, Levi's sentiments. Although conversations were a bit one-sided, as partners they got along well with these dynamics in place.

That was all he had to say and left the air quiet until Tam decided to speak.

"My name is Tam. I am one of the founders of the Greater London Investigators of the Paranormal, otherwise known as GLIP. I have been tracking and recording strange phenomenon all my life. Some people would call me a 'ghost chaser,' but I've experienced all kinds of manifestations. I must be honest when I say that I am not too sure just how much my team can help you as we are mostly about detecting and recording strange events, but we are open-minded and here to help."

Simon and Gareth also gave their brief introductions and then everyone turned toward the elderly man at the table.

"My name is Walter Smith, but long ago my name was Walter Schmitt. I was born in Germany and during World War II, my rank was Obergruppenfuhrer, which is similar in rank to a Lieutenant General. Heinrich Himmler appointed me to head up a secret detachment of SS soldiers, with the blessing of Adolf Hitler. My task was a simple one. I had to create a program by which to kill as many of the opposing sides as possible.

I received a relic known as the Heilige Lanze, or Holy Lance, to aid me in completing my mission. You might know this lance by its more popular name, Spear of Destiny. Historically, this lance stabbed Jesus as he hung on the cross, according to the Gospel of John. Hitler had found it in Austria during the Anschluss, or annexation of Austria, and had it sent to Nuremburg. He had a replica made, later returned to Austria by invading allied forces after the war. American General George S. Patton believed he had the genuine relic when he returned it to Austria, but the factual one was made available to me for use in my task. To make a long story short, I used a combination of arcane magic, science, and the relic to create a weapon. My weapon was ten thousand men that could transmit their bodies through the atmosphere, like radio waves, and reach a target they could kill.

My plan was two-fold. One part was to kill as many of the British as I could since they were our greatest stationary threat. You see, although the Russians were almost upon us in the spring of 1945, we could not fix on a specific target due to their moving army. We reasoned that a fixed location with a heavy population, like London, would be best. The second part of my plan was just overall disruption. I figured that even if my manifestations of SS soldiers did make it to London, I had no guarantee they would have enough corporal matter to inflict damage. I hoped that just by their appearance I would create a demoralizing affect on the British."

The GLIP members, shocked by what they had just heard, had a hard time believing it. Tam asked many clarifying questions and finally ended with the one that stumped even Walter.

"So why now? How come your 'manifestations,' as you called them are appearing now and not back in 1945 like they were supposed to?"

Shadowfall

Walter's blank expression changed into a slight smile as he replied.

"I have no idea. I was sort of hoping that you, the so-called 'experts,' might have an idea."

The group sat quietly, a little intimidated by the snarky sounding comment. It was a tense moment before Walter commenced.

"Look, I know the secret location. I know how I set things up. Something must have changed or been altered in some way. I think that we need to get to the right spot and see what's there. I assume you are here for your expertise in dealing with the supernatural. Your detecting and monitoring equipment might come in useful, perhaps, but ultimately it will be up to me to end the manifestations."

There was a little more discussion, and then a map of Germany underwent extensive examination. The map showed the Black Forest was about four-hundred and seventy-five miles from their present location. It would take them a minimum of seven to eight hours to drive there. They decided not to hire a helicopter, as they were not to draw attention to themselves; everyone would run the risk of letting this night go by to get some sleep before the journey. They agreed to go to sleep now and get up at midnight for the trek by mini-van. Levi and Deron would drive affording the team more sleep if they desired while driving.

Before turning in, Tam, Simon, and Gareth held their own short conference. Tam admitted she was worried and had no idea what they could do to help, but since they were here, she felt committed to do her best. Simon and Gareth agreed. She also did not understand why the

Israelis and an ex-Nazi were working together, but she reasoned aloud that if that is what it takes to end the invasion in London, then so be it. They checked their equipment to make sure all was in working order and went to their rooms to sleep, with Levi and Deron on-guard in the main room that connected the suite.

Chapter Twelve

Back in London, the authorities were perplexed about the whole situation. They had no leads as the Israelis decided not to share what little information they had until they could figure it out themselves. Even so, Tamir Pardo was the only one that really knew what was going on; even he did not believe it. Sending Walter and the GLIP team with some of his operatives was mostly for fact-finding in his mind. He figured Smith would stop the actions, whatever they were, or he wouldn't. If he didn't, his Mossad operatives had the power to use their own judgment. For now Pardo was taking the 'wait and see' approach to this unusual problem.

Tam had left several directives for the GLIP members; at least for any that didn't quit after the chaos of the Roman House Apartments. Her directive was simply to assist the authorities as needed. Local police had in fact gone to the GLIP headquarters shortly after Tam, Simon, and Gareth left in order to solicit any help they could get. Every team member available was outfitted with an EMF meter, two-way radio, digital thermometer, and a full-spectrum camera. Due to the limitations of the GLIP resources, this amounted to six members, and each assigned to their respective authorities around the perimeter of London. Their task was to give warning if they noticed something and to record as much as they could with the equipment.

Because of the widespread damage of the night before, a general notice was posted on poles and walls and transmitted through local radio and television, for Londoners to seek evening's lodgings outside of London proper. This was not a mandatory order, but an advisement. A few people took the advice and left the city, but only about one of every four people. Many, especially the older people, felt that if they could live through the London bombings of World War II, they could get through this situation too.

Besides the advisement, everything else seemed normal outdoors during the late afternoon. All of the effects of a slowly sinking-in panic were happening behind closed doors; which had been bolted and barricaded out of fear. There were many rumors running around and one of them was that the Nazi-ghosts were using television transmissions to get into people's homes. Many Londoners unplugged their televisions before dusk and some even heaved them out of windows, just to be on the safe side. Some citizens were arming themselves or at the very least putting on makeshift armor. By nightfall, the streets were empty except for roving police patrol vehicles.

The tensions were supplanted around eight o'clock as the terror started.

The invasion occurred all at once; in every household simultaneously. The nightly apparitions of dead Nazi soldiers materialized quickly and sought the total destruction of any inhabitants they found. Bodies were being thrown through upper level windows; people were running out of their homes trailing blood behind them, some missing body parts that had been cut off. Babies were crying until they were stopped short and never heard from again. Fires broke out as the citizens fought back against their attackers using whatever they could find including gasoline or other combustibles. Instead of barking, dogs were fleeing the downtown area in droves.

Police phone lines were flooded instantly as people sought assistance of one kind or another. Dispatch operators were hearing similar things from each person that called.

"Police, please report your problem."

"Help me! He's after me! I ran into another room, but he's trying to kick down the door!"

"Who's after you?"

"One of them ghosts! He has eyes as black as coal! Help me, quickly!"

"Try to calm down Miss and give me your address."

Sounds of a door splitting over the phone line...

"Help me! Help! He has my kitchen knife! My arm! No! Please stop...Arrrrrggghhh!"

Silence.

Some dispatchers claimed to hear occasional exclamations in German. With all calls recorded, everyone made their best effort to determine the locations of callers, but the police tactical maps were soon awash in dotted coverage. The entire City of London had lit up like a Christmas tree in just the first three minutes of the invasion.

In every household where some living person was present, the same story repeated itself. The Nazi-ghosts just materialized out of the ether and started attacking.

People claimed later that they felt the blows; grabbed, punched, kicked, or even hit by other objects the ghosts wielded, but everyone agreed the ghosts felt nothing in return. Survivors agreed with the fact their own fists and weapons just passed harmlessly through the unflinching ghosts. Attempts to record the ghosts on video or with cameras were futile, as the ghosts were nearly invisible on film; at best, they showed as a smudge or shadow.

The Nazi-ghost invasion lasted only fifteen minutes this time, but it was enough to leave thousands dead or dying. Emergency crews could not keep up with the demand for assistance. Unaccounted people were later discovered deceased; unable to crawl out of their own barricaded flats where they had bled to death from their injuries. Once things quieted down and with several hours to go before dawn, the surviving Londoners started fleeing en masse. Citizens were using cars, motorcycles, bicycles, or even just walking out of town. Any who were still sane in the aftermath of the attack had had enough and were leaving.

That morning would find the hospitals and morgues overflowing. Makeshift hospitals and morgues were temporarily established. Reporters from all around were flocking to London to see what they could uncover, but the authorities smartly decided to blockade London and not let anyone in. For all purposes, authorities were treating London as if it were under quarantine from this point on. Press conferences occurred only at the edge of the city. Priests that came from far away to administer blessings were forbidden to go into downtown areas. The sun dawned on streets littered with the fleeing, the dying, and the dead.

Chapter Thirteen

Gareth couldn't sleep during the long car ride to the Black Forest. He knew he should focus on the mission at hand, but all he could do was wonder if he and Tam would ever get together. He didn't like that Simon was on this adventure with them, but he also knew Simon had infinitely more experience with the supernatural than he did. He reasoned he was lucky to be here at all, and only his jealous outburst made them take him too. *I will have to step up my efforts to remind Tam I am interested in being with her. I need to handle myself professionally and try to impress Tam.*

Simon and Tam slept peacefully on the bench seat next to him as all of their gear and bags took up the rest of the minivan, except for one seat behind him for Walter. Gareth looked at them and noticed Tam's head was resting on Simon's shoulder. She had a smile of contentment on her face. Gareth wondered if maybe he should back off. Tam seemed to like Simon a lot. Gareth turned away and looked out the window at all of the passing trees and road and before he knew it, he drifted off to sleep.

Around 8:30 in the morning, Simon and Gareth awoke because of the car's speedy rhythm slowing down. The motions they felt indicated they were getting off the highway and pulling in somewhere. Gareth opened his eyes and saw they were pulling into a courtyard with a small café. Gareth looked at Simon and saw that Tam was still asleep with her head still on his shoulder, but also she now had her arm wrapped around his arm. Simon saw he was looking at Tam and decided it meant he should awake her. Simon shook her a little and said; "Tam...Darling...wakey, wakey...Time to get up. The show is at hand." Tam opened her eyes and looked up at Simon and smiled and hugged his arm tighter before letting go and sitting up to assess the situation. Gareth shuddered inwardly.

For Mossad covert operatives, Levi and Deron were realistic taskmasters. They timed breaks perfectly for restroom or eating time. This would be both as they had been on the road so long. They all exited the minivan and went into the café. Gareth managed to get ahead of Simon and held the door open for Tam hoping she might think of him as a gentleman. Inside, they all sat down, ordered, and ate breakfast in silence. Deron had brought in his laptop to check for news on London. He picked one article and read aloud.

Nazi Invasion Continues!
Associated Press –London

Last night Londoners were again besieged by what appear to be Nazi ghosts. The assaults have been occurring over the last few nights and start at various times after sundown. Londoners are taking to the streets in fear as they claim to be pursued by these apparitions from the past. The death toll has been rising nightly. The events of the evening before accounted for only a few dozen deaths. Last evenings barrage was the worst yet with 5,128 confirmed dead and an equal number injured. At this time, local authorities have no idea what is causing this outbreak and are encouraging people to seek lodgings outside of London. Although there is a mass exodus of citizens fleeing the city, it is not yet mandatory to do so. Many citizens fear further invasions in the evening time. Local paranormal investigators have declined to comment any further on events.

There were many other accounts of the events from last night, some with graphic details, but the group had gotten the information they needed. Whatever was happening...it was still going on. The group also realized the problem was escalating from a few dozen dead the night before, to over five-thousand killed last night. None of the group said it aloud, but they all wondered what might happen if another night passes.

Everyone ate quickly and headed back to the minivan. On the way back, Gareth felt a hand on his shoulder and he turned and faced Walter. Out of earshot of the others, Walter told him, "If you like the girl let her know as soon as possible. It can't hurt and it may bring you two together. If she didn't notice you before, she will have to think about you after she knows you like her." Gareth looked at Walter with a shocked expression and muttered, "What are you talking about? I was just..." Walter gave Gareth a sly look of knowing and said, "I see the way you look at her. The first thing you must do is to just accept that you like her." With that, Walter took his hand off Gareth's shoulder and got in the car. Gareth hesitated for a moment to internalize what the old man had told him and then piled in too.

Shadowfall

They drove on and Levi told them they were getting very close to their destination, but the last few miles required trekking by foot, as the area Walter had indicated was quite remote. In another hour, they entered the Black Forest at the town of Freiburg and took rooms at a hotel from where they would head out to the secret area indicated by Walter Schmitt...now Smith. They quickly changed into hiking gear and the GLIP members made sure that all of their equipment fit into their backpacks.

Levi and Deron held a quick meeting in which they told everyone that the hotel rooms were the rendezvous point if anyone got separated from the group. They also made sure everyone had a card with contact numbers in the event any of them was incapacitated and they needed help. Whereas the Mossad agents had held onto all of their documents up until this point, they now handed over temporary identification and Israeli diplomatic visas to everyone in the group in case officials stopped them.

Simon spoke up and asked about weapons. The agents told them that only they would be carrying weapons. This was a fact-finding mission and not an operation. Weapons were never part of the deal. The group was here to help using their ghost-hunting equipment and recording whatever events transpired.

The group headed out for their hike and blended in with all of the other tourists going out for hikes. The sun was up and the air was crisp with hints of spruce and pine wafting through the air. Many footpaths led to the Black Forest, and the group followed Deron onto one of these.

The history of the Black Forest region included mining. On the hike out, Walter confided that it was an old iron ore mine where his detachment of SS soldiers operated. Gareth noticed how spry the man was for his age and marveled at his stamina. Walter had no trouble hiking. He wasn't fast, but he kept up a good, solid pace.

"Walter, you are a marvel. I can't believe your energy," said Tam aloud, "We can barely keep up with you!"

Without missing a step, Walter told them he had always been in good shape. His years with the Hitler Youth had taught him about eating healthy and exercise. His years of hiding after the war taught him to go without luxuries. Walter told them about how he worked in vineyards clear up until recently. Walter also told them he did enjoy beer and wine in moderation and even enjoyed an occasional cigar, as long as it was Cuban.

Levi and Deron rarely talked to the others, except as necessary. Their objective was to help the ex-Nazi and these so-called 'experts' to get to their location and do what they have to do. They were to assist and protect the group, but not get involved outside of protecting them. They were debriefed on what the mission was all about and told that if things went awry, they were allowed to use their own judgment in regards to the final outcome – even if that meant the deaths of all involved. The operatives did not care what the others talked about as long as they were not discussing Mossad or Israeli secrets and were moving on toward their objective. They carried guns, knives, and some small munitions, but kept these on their bodies and out of sight from the others.

The party walked several miles along a footpath into the Black Forest. There were footpaths all over the forest and hikers had luckily taken other routes. The route that the party stayed on seemed seldom used. Tam wondered if maybe the phenomena in the area somehow kept people from wanting to venture this way. She, herself, felt a sense of dread creeping up on her, but she kept it secret. *No need to worry everyone else*, she thought. Little did she know that everyone was experiencing the same sensation, but no one said anything about it. After what seemed like a hike of much more than a couple of miles, Walter stopped them.

"We're near the entrance. Let's get off the path and set up a temporary camp. There's a clearing at the bottom of a valley on the other side of that hill to our left. No one from the path will see us, or hear us, as long as we're quiet. We used to post guards there during the war." No one contested Walter. This was his show. Everyone knew he was the key to stopping whatever was going on. Tam thought they were lucky he was still alive to help stop the supernatural invasion. She just hoped everything would work out all right.

The group easily found the valley, climbed down to the bottom, and set up one large tent for the six of them. It would be close quarters, thought Gareth, but he would make an effort to lie next to Tam and maybe try to share some of his feelings with her if they got a chance to relax...later on. The GLIP members also set up their equipment and got prepared to monitor the surrounding area. They were not prepared for what they recorded on their equipment.

Chapter Fourteen

The GLIP members were busy getting out and setting up their equipment as the Mossad operatives did a quick sweep of the immediate area. Gareth and Simon set up their unique equipment; the EVP (electronic voice phenomena) recorders, digital thermometers to watch fluctuations in temperature that might signal an approaching apparition, and several EMF (electromagnetic field) meters. Tam's task was to set up a few full spectrum digital camcorders with motion detectors, mounted on tripods around the camp, but ready for easy detachment if they needed to take them elsewhere.

Luckily, ghost-hunting equipment was smaller and more efficient now than the stuff investigators used even a decade ago. The only power source needed now was a long-lasting battery or place to plug in. Everything had easily fit in their backpacks and had been lightweight enough for the hike. Levi and Deron had their backpacks full with water, energy bars, and some military-type dry rations to share with the group as needed. It was just about ten in the morning when the team had everything set up. Walter seemed anxious for them to hurry and turn everything on. Tam inspected how everything was set up and then gave the command to turn it all on.

Immediately every instrument pegged in the red. The digital thermometers showed fluctuations on temperature by as much as ten degrees every few seconds. The digital camcorders appeared to detect motion. The EMF meters quickly overloaded and blew.

"Damn it! We don't have any more EMF meters!" Tam yelled out. Simon responded with some reason, "I don't think we need them anymore. There's obviously a heavy amount of electro-magnetic activity going on here." Tam turned and gave Simon an angry look and was just about to say something when Gareth smiled at Tam and spoke up, "Why don't we see what the video camera is picking up?"

Tam hadn't turned on the monitor yet. She walked over, switched it on, and slumped into a seating position on the ground in front of the screen. Simon, Gareth, and Walter all crowded around her to see what they could see. Levi and Deron kept watch and seemed disinterested in what they were doing. The screen came on.

"Oh, my God!" exclaimed Tam, her sentiment shared by the others viewing the screen.

On the screen were ghostly images of young men in Nazi uniforms. Some were walking around and appeared to be examining the group. Some appeared to try to attack the group with fists, but no one felt anything. Although they appeared as if they were superimposed images on the screen, they were all well defined. You could see the men well, although ghostly. All of the men had one other thing in common; they all had black eyes, just the same as witnessed before. You could see the features on their faces, but their eyes were solid black on the screen and unblinking. They had a liquid appearance, like oil tar.

Shadowfall

"Henri, Gunther, Bruno, Helmut...Gerhard...Lars..." whispered Walter as tears began welling up in his eyes and he appeared to shiver. Just then, one of the ghost-men stared from the monitor and it blinked out. Simon tried to turn it back on, but nothing happened.

Simon turned to look at Walter and said, "Walter, what happened just now? Do you know these guys? Look...last night we were too stunned by what you were telling us even to believe you. We believe you now. I don't think any of us are really equipped to deal with . . . apparitions. You need to explain exactly what you did to these men. If we're lucky, maybe we can free them by undoing whatever it is that you did."

Walter wiped his tears with his hands and looked at the group.

"I don't know how they destroyed your monitor, but I would guess they can't harm us under sunlight. To answer your other question, yes...I know...I knew those men. They were some of the best under my command. It's hard to see them like this after so many years. I had hoped they had all found peace in their graves. I never expected to see them as undead creatures solely bent on unleashing their hatred and violence after all these decades." He broke off as tears welled up in his eyes again.

Tam stood up, put her hand on his shoulder, and said, "We can tell this is hard for you, but please remember people are dying everyday because of these beings. What did you do to them? You need to tell us. How did you make them like this?"

Walter wiped his tears again and straightened up before speaking again.

"It was the spring of 1945. Hitler had ordered Himmler to take the Spear of Destiny and entrust it to me. You see, I had pitched my plan to him some months earlier and out of desperation, he was looking to the occult as a means by which to help him turn the tide and win the war. Assigned to an old iron ore mine here in the Black Forest, I was allotted a detachment of 10,000 SS soldiers. Inside the mine, I constructed a large Drudenfuss from a large central cavern. In English, it would be Druid's Foot, but you probably call it a pentagram. Utilized in ancient times to ward off evil spirits, but it can also bind them. This Drudenfuss, or pentagram, is made out of metal, locking boxes that are tied together with tubing. At the center of the pentagram is a cistern that contains an ichor substance of my own creation.

"The black liquid ichor flows from the cistern to all of the boxes, each containing one of my soldiers. Much like the science-fiction idea of suspended animation, except through eldritch means, my soldiers suffered a dream-like state; half between consciousness and unconsciousness, suspended in the black tar-like liquid. The combined spiritual energy from my soldiers transferred to the Spear of Destiny placed directly in the middle of the pentagram on top of the cistern. I alluded to transmitting my men before…The spear is the transmitter. As the energy flows into it, it displaces time and space by some phenomena of occult working called Schattenzauber, or shadow magic. The spear then transmits spiritual energy through the ionosphere to wherever directed; much like the transmission of an AM radio signal. Since the ionosphere is somehow critical to making the transmission, it only allows for maximum effect at night. That is probably why the men we saw trying to attack us, could not harm us with the sun overhead. In any case, I created incantations that tuned the location to that of London since I needed a fixed point for transmission.

"Everything was set, and I had just placed the spear in position and opened the valves to allow the flow of ichor when we were alerted that the Russians had entered Berlin and that our Fuhrer, Hitler, had committed suicide. One of our last dispatches from Berlin instructed us to destroy all sign of our operations and escape by means of a program called Operation Werewolf. A colonel by the name of Maximilian Hartmann was to be given the spear for 'safe keeping.' This order was signed by Hitler himself on April 30th, just a few days before and must have been one of his last wishes. Well, this Hartmann arrived with two of his officers on the same day we received the dispatch and wanted to leave quickly with the spear wrapped up in canvas."

"So your operation didn't work? You said you started it. What happened?"

"Using occult energy takes time and a great deal of energy. Once I started the process, I saw eldritch gasses of a greenish color passing from the men in the boxes and flowing into the spear. The spear started glowing and a single ray was starting to grow outward from the top of it. We watched it grow until it reached the top of the cavern and finally appeared to pass through it. Our guards outside notified us when it appeared over the mountain that our tunnels were in. This ray kept growing and was reaching towards the west; toward

England. I knew our mission was going to work and I hoped to pull it off before Colonel Hartmann arrived. Alas, he did arrive and, we had to pull away the spear, and that ended the ray, aborting our task. As far as I ever knew, London was safe…until now."

"But what happened to your men?"

"Hartmann told us to follow our instructions immediately. He assumed that the men in the boxes were all dead, or would soon be dead, by drowning in the ichor and I could not convince him otherwise. Hartmann made us set the charges to blow the caverns and tunnels, holding me at gunpoint for my outbursts. Hartmann had all of my men lined up and shot with the exception of my two most senior officers. Luckily, these men were on my side and I am hoping they set the charges to blow only the main entrance as they signaled me they would. The explosion satisfied Hartmann and he drove off immediately thereafter taking me along with him and his officers, still at gunpoint. My two officers remained behind with instructions to destroy whatever was left and then themselves. I never found out whatever became of them. I didn't care what was going to happen to me. For some reason I wanted to go wherever the spear was going. I know now the evil contained within the spear is what drew me to it as someone who knew how to harness its powers."

"So what happened to you and the spear?"

Walter gave out a low chuckle before replying; "I was forced to follow Colonel Hartmann and his two other men. We left Germany in such a dizzying escape through back alleys, tunnels, waterways…I cannot remember it all. I thought Hartmann brought me along because I was important; I knew how to use the spear. I was wrong. I think at first he believed I was important to the Fuhrer and to Germany, but as it got tougher and tougher for the four of us to get around, he eventually grew tired of all of us. Luckily, for me he did arrange through the men running Operation Werewolf to smuggle us into Argentina with forged documents that had been prepared in advance.

Once we touched foot in South America, he disappeared. He took the Spear of Destiny and just disappeared one night leaving the rest of us to fend for ourselves on the streets of a foreign country. None of us spoke any Spanish, but at least we were out of our uniforms. The underground network that smuggled us out had provided regular clothing along with our new identities. After a few days of dodging in and out of doorways, trying to steal what little food we could, and sleeping in culverts, the other two officers left me and went off on their own. Later, I learned these men died.

I used my wits to survive. I played mute until I learned a bit of the language and took every terrible job I could find. I stayed away from the occult. My mind was just a whirlwind of confusion after my failed mission, subsequent escape from Europe, and the fall of Germany. I took solace in work. Like the famous words we Germans used during the war, 'Arbeit macht frei'... 'Work will set you free.' I took refuge in ignorance. I shed the life of Obergruppenfuhrer Walter Schmitt and became just plain Walter Smith instead. And now, after many years I am forced back into remembering a life that I had hoped was forgotten for all time."

"Let me get this straight. In all these years...decades...you never heard anything more about your mission, Hartmann, or the spear?"

"No. Not a thing. I was happy it never came back to haunt me, until now. I am so old that it hardly matters. That is another lucky break for me. I am here to try to figure out why my mission is working now and end it. If all goes well, I hope for anonymity once again ...after all this is over. I just want to go back to the vineyards and my pleasant valley in Argentina where the sea rises to meet the sun and time is forgotten."

"Okay. That is a beautiful thought, but what is our first move?"

Walter chuckled again, and said, "We go inside of course."

Chapter Fifteen

Walter explained to the group that while the main entrance had been blown up, there was a smaller, secret entrance only officers had known about. He intimated he was certain his trusted officers would have left this entrance intact for an eventuality such as Walter returning. He tried to tell everyone about the loyalty his men felt for him, but it fell on deaf ears. Everyone in the group was preoccupied with thoughts about what they might find and how they fit into all of this. They thought about how they would actually be of any help. Even Levi and Deron, as stoic as they were, seemed lost in thought.

The party gathered all of their equipment and hiked half a mile further into the northern end of the small valley where they were located. There was a pile of boulders at this end, Walter climbed about halfway up and disappeared behind one. He was gone for only a minute, but it seemed to make the Mossad operatives nervous and they were about to follow where he had gone. Walter's reemergence stopped them. He told everyone he found the secret exit, just as he remembered it. He bade them to follow him and he waited until they were near him before proceeding. Just as he turned to go behind the boulder again, Tam reached out her arm and touched his. He stopped and looked at her and said, "Yes?"

"Walter, I'm still not even sure why GLIP was brought into this. Even if we get inside, are we going to really be of any help to you?"

He looked into Tam's eyes and smiled.

"Maybe you are part of an elaborate joke created by my jailer, Mr. Pardo. I don't know. I guess he figures you know enough about the supernatural to either assist me or at least bear witness and record what I do. Maybe you should have your video cameras and other necessary equipment turned on."

The GLIP members took this as a cue, silently took out their equipment, and turned it all on. Tam had made sure each member had a small full-spectrum camera they could wear on headbands or hats and they put these on. Levi and Deron moved to different positions. Levi stayed behind everyone, bringing up the rear, and Deron climbed just ahead of Walter and told him that he would take the lead into the tunnels.

The group slid in between some boulders and followed a flow of cool air blowing from deep within the pile of boulders. At some points, they had to lay on their bellies and use hands and feet to crawl any further. *I'm glad no one seems to be claustrophobic, although it would be nice to comfort Tam if she was*, thought Gareth.

After crawling and wiggling through the rocks for about ten minutes, the group finally reached an aperture that emptied onto a small cavern, just big enough for the six members of the group to stand in. The GLIP team turned on their LED lights and the Mossad operatives, Levi and Deron, each pulled out a Beretta Model 70 .22 caliber long rifle pistols. They did not have any lights,

Shadowfall

but they affixed laser-targeting lights on their pistols. Walter, like GLIP, had a headband LED that he put on.

With their lights on, they could see this small cavern had a lot of cobwebs and Tam gasped as she saw some big spiders scurrying away from the light. She grabbed Simon's hand and gasped. Simon looked at her and patted her hand and said, "It's okay Tam. Just some spiders...look...They are trying to get away from us. We'll be fine." Gareth felt miserable at the sight of seeing Tam holding Simon's hand and thought he might as well get used to the fact Tam will never be his. Tam told the group she was sorry for her outburst, but spiders always gave her a start. She told everyone she would be fine now. Now that she knew to expect them.

Checking the cavern, the group could see a narrow tunnel leading out of this small cavern. Walter told them it wound into the mountain and would eventually end in a solid metal wall that he knew how to open. Deron led the way through the small tunnel. The tunnel had many turns to the right and left and sometimes dipped down or rose up. As the team moved on, the tunnel became more damp and the walls were increasingly covered in lichen. At some junctures, the team had to wade through water to proceed on. Within a few minutes, they came to the solid metal wall of which Walter had told them. It was made of overlapping sheets of iron and bolts. Walter bent down, put one hand on the bottom right hand panel, and pushed it while using his other hand to turn a nearby bolt. The metal section pushed inward and created a doorway about three-feet tall by three-feet wide to crawl through. It was dark inside and even bending down with lights did not show what was ahead.

"There's nothing to worry about. This was a secret exit only officers knew about, and built before any soldiers arrived. This panel will lead us into a large storage shed. From there, we will be in the main cavern and we will see once and for all what is happening with my creation…after all these years." Walter sounded excited and maybe a little enthusiastic. Tam wondered if he had really repented of his past deeds as a Nazi or not. Simon just figured he was thrilled to revisit his past, no matter how gruesome. Gareth thought the old man might just be happy to get this all over with and was anxious to close this chapter of his life finally. Walter had mixed emotions. On one hand, he would be excited to see that his sorcery worked and he did share occult power like his mother before him, but he was also excited to get this over and return to his beloved Argentina. Walter sounded impatient as he motioned to Deron to proceed and said, "Let's go."

Deron went in first, gun out in front of him. Walter followed, then everyone else, with Levi in the rear. They left the panel open behind them and found themselves in a large metal shed as Walter had told them. Inside the room were various tools, all covered in a patina of dust. There was only one door out of the storage shed and Deron went and tried it and found it locked from the outside. Walter told him the officers always kept it locked except when tools were called for. After a brief discussion between Walter and the GLIP team, they decided they would have to try to shoot at the padlock from this side. Levi told them not to worry as he stepped forward and took out what looked like a large laser pointer. He told Walter to aim his headband light on the section of the door where they could see the lock hasp. Then Levi turned on the laser and cut through the hasp. All heard the lock fall to the floor and with a quick turn of a metal handle, the door was open.

Deron was first to step through into the massive cavern. Everyone followed his lead and quickly exited the shed to see what was there. The cavern was so huge and vast that the headband LEDs did not penetrate far enough in and it was difficult to make out shapes ahead. There was an eerie greenish-glow coming from the horizon ahead.

"There were once great generators that provided electricity, but I doubt those work now. We should just move ahead and see what is going on. The only thing ahead is the pentagram of boxes and the cistern I told you about. The men's quarters and equipment were kept in other tunnels running off from this cavern," said Walter, who was growing ever more anxious, "Let's keep moving."

Deron walked ahead with Walter directly behind him. After Walter were Tam and Simon and then Gareth with Levi bringing up the rear. As they neared the green glow, they began to make out the shape of large metal boxes. These boxes appeared old and grimy, covered with the dust of decades, yet the glow seemed to come from the top of them. The party passed over what appeared to be a concrete curb that curved off to the right and left of them in an inward arc.

As the party passed this boundary, the damp air felt colder. Tam and Simon stopped, as if by instinct, and turned on their digital thermometers before moving on. Tam whispered, "The temperature is dropping steadily as we get closer." Simon told Gareth to turn on his full-spectrum video camera and keep an eye on the view screen. As soon as Gareth turned it on and looked, he saw a large ghostly image of a man moving towards them from the direction of the boxes.

"Uh, guys...There is an apparition moving toward us rather quickly."

Everyone looked forward and saw nothing. "It probably can't harm us here, like the apparitions we saw outside," Simon said. Everyone was still looking forward when Deron's body appeared to float in the air. His legs were kicking violently as he squeezed the trigger of his gun repeatedly into nothingness. Only a faint shadow stood directly in front of him. Through the video camera viewer screen, Gareth saw what was happening and told the others. "He's being choked by a large uniformed man! Deron's bullets have passed through him!" That was all he had time to say as Levi leapt at the shadow, but passed through it like the bullets had. He seemed stunned for a few seconds until he managed to get back on his feet. Deron's eyes were bulging, and he had dropped his pistol. He was clutching at his neck with both hands, with his body still suspended in the air by a pair of strong ghost hands. Deron's last words were a feeble wheeze, "Run!"

Chapter Sixteen

Levi not knowing what to do, but remembered his mission was to protect Walter and the others, ran back to them; leaving Deron twitching his last in the air behind him. He ran straight to Walter, picked him up, and ran him back to the shed. Tam, Simon, and Gareth all followed him. As Tam ran blindly toward the shed, she had forgotten about the concrete curb that they had stepped over before. She caught her foot and fell flat on the ground. Her whole body was past the curb except for her right foot and ankle. She struggled to get up, but felt something icy cold wrapped around her ankle and was starting to pull her back over the curb. She screamed. Gareth stayed closely behind Tam, and saw her fall. He immediately grabbed both her hands and tried to pull her forward, but something was holding her fast. There was a tense few seconds as Gareth tried with all his might to pull her forward while she was slowly being pulled back toward the area of the boxes. Simon made the difference. He ran back and grabbed Tam around the mid-section and together he and Gareth had enough strength to pull her loose from the icy grip of her unseen assailant and over the curb. With Tam between them and her arms around their shoulders, they helped her to the shed.

Once in the shed, they closed the door behind them. Panting, Levi asked Walter; "Are we safe here or do we need to get to sunlight?" Walter looked up at him and with a look of remorse told him; "I'm truly sorry about your partner. I thought we would be safe. We are safe here. You see, the soldiers cannot leave the pentagram. They are bound to it. They can only leave by means of the spear, and only if it is in place."

Simon grabbed Walter and shook him. He said, "What else have you forgotten to tell us? We told you we're not equipped to handle this situation, but we're stuck with you! We're stuck, but we are willing to help you, right guys?" He looked at Tam and Gareth and they both nodded in the affirmative. "So, look mate, what else should we know?" He let go of Walter and waited for a reply.

"Yes. It is only right to tell you a few things. If you remember, I told you the boxes form a giant pentagram. As long as you are on the outside of the pentagram, you are safe. If you cross it, the soldiers can harm you. I don't know exactly how it works, but the men are only undead shadows of themselves, ghosts if you prefer, except within the pentagram and wherever the Spear of Destiny directs them. In these instances, they can will their extremities into definitiveness and hit, kick, grab, and so on."

This time Levi stepped forward and asked if there were anything else. Walter thought for a minute and added; "I don't think they can harm me as my blood, was used as a base to create the ichor, but I could be wrong. I never had to test that theory of occult workings. In addition, out there, I did not notice if the spear was in place. There should have been a shaft of green light emanating from the cistern. Without the staff, these soldiers and their life force should not be able to leave the pentagram. Something is not right here."

The group slumped down in the shed and caught their breath. Gareth, who had been helping Tam stay upright on her legs, helped her to sit and inspected her ankle. It felt extremely cold and there were deep bruises forming which resembled finger marks. Tam said she was okay, it hurt a bit, but nothing was broken and she should be able to walk soon. Gareth started rubbing her ankle trying to warm it and make it feel better. No one could see Tam blush in the low light, but she felt a bit unnerved over this attention and told Gareth quietly to stop. Gareth went on rubbing as if he were in a trance until Tam finally pulled her leg back and told him loudly to stop. "Tam, I'm just trying to help." Gareth said with some embarrassment. "I'm fine!" was Tam's only rejoinder. Simon placed his hands on Gareth's shoulders and said to him, "We all know you mean well. It's cool, right Tam?" Tam looked up at the pair. Simon had turned Gareth to face Tam and now had his arm slung around Gareth's shoulder. Tam smiled at the two and said, "Sure. No problem. Teammates help each other. No hard feelings."

Levi looked at Walter and addressed him, "Walter, we're here to stop whatever is going on that's affecting the citizens of London. We've made it here and see that your 'handiworks' are still in place. Now I ask you, what do we do now? What can we do to stop these undead shades for all time?"

Walter leaned back against the wall and closed his eyes before speaking. "I'm not too sure. Since I do not see the staff, I would assume these spirits are trapped here, bound by the pentagram. We cannot simply destroy the pentagram. That would just free their force to roam anywhere with their power intact. We must reverse the flow of ichor back into the cistern and undo incantations with further incantations, which I am not sure if I remember correctly as I am so old and have given up all occult knowledge and readings these last seven decades since the end of the war."

"Look, my partner died out there just now at the hand of one of your creations. You must tell me what to do to terminate these beings and help me end all of this. I will admit, at first I did not believe in any of this, but I do now, and I vowed to avenge my partner and stop Nazis, especially supernatural ones. There must be something I can do?" Walter looked at Levi and felt sympathy for his passion. He remembered what passion like that felt like. He remembered once being young, robust, and full of energy and confidence and being eager to take on the world. Walter also wanted to end this and end it now. He dreamed of getting back to his vineyards and his lazy and carefree life in Argentina. He wanted to get death and hatred behind him once again. He could only say; "Let me think for a moment." He thought back through the decades and tried to drag up all the arcane and eldritch knowledge he could remember from his mother and from his own learning. Eventually an idea came to him.

"I think I have it. Do you remember when I told you the creatures might not harm me as my blood, my life force, mixes with theirs? What we do is I take the lead and all of you walk directly behind me. The person behind me puts their hands on my waist as we walk and each person does likewise to the person in front of them.

Sort of like a conga line. In this way, we are all connected to each other. All of you will connect to my aura, which is what these creatures probably detect. We get to the cistern and reverse the flow of the fluid that binds and connects them all. In this way, they will have no power and we can undo the pentagram with my incantations."

"Why do you need all of us? If they won't harm you, why don't you go by yourself?"

"I wish I could. The cistern is manual. Since it was built on a raised area at the center of the cavern, also the center of the pentagram, the fluid was able to flow to the men in the boxes with no problem. The pumps that can pump the fluid back into the cistern are manual and rather large. Two separate pumps work in tandem. It will take two strong people at each pump to reverse the flow. I can assist, but I am probably too weak now to run one by myself."

Tam voiced her thoughts. "We all came here together, and we will solve this together. We might not understand the occult very well, but we understand hard work. You can count on us, right guys?" She looked at Gareth and Simon who nodded and voiced their agreement. "Besides, we live in London and we can't return knowing we didn't try our best to help our friends, family, and neighbors to the best of our abilities."

"But are you willing to give up your life, if necessary?"

Tam was shaken by what Walter said, but decided he was being more figurative rather than literal and said, "Yes, absolutely."

Walter gave her a little smile and then shared the smile around the group and said, "I guess we have nothing left to do except to get this over with then."

The group decided to leave behind all of their equipment. The GLIP members reasoned that their ghost hunting equipment was a waste here and all they needed was their muscle and wits. Levi checked his gun and holstered it, but kept it with him. Walter left his knapsack too and everything he had except his clothing and his headlamp for light. He worried if his memory would hold. He tried going over the necessary incantations in his mind and kept double guessing himself. He knew the final incantations had to be correct.

The group walked to the boundary curb and then lined up with Walter at the lead. Tam was behind Walter, then Simon, then Gareth, and finally Levi. They all placed their hands on the hips or shoulders or the person in front of them and on a cue from Walter began walking over the curb and into the pentagram. As they approached the old iron boxes for the second time, and saw the green glow emanating from the tops again, they could make out a few shadows moving in the eldritch light. First one shadow started coming toward them, then two more, then a few others. They no longer needed the video camera screen to see them as their eyes had adjusted to the darkness of the cavern. They appeared to move straight at Walter, but nothing happened. The group kept walking slowly as Walter reminded them not to break contact with one another, not even to scratch a nose.

With great caution, the group advanced slowly toward the cistern. They started passing rows of the connected metal boxes that seemed to curve off to the right and left of them into darkness, further than they could see. All the while, about a dozen malevolent shadows seemed to float around them. The air was thick with hatred and malice, but no attack happened. The air got colder and damper as they pressed on.

Looking down as they passed every row of boxes, the group had to carefully pick their way over heavy black tubing that connected each box to another. The green gaseous glow that emanated from each metal box came from the top of the box where there was a pane of glass that showed the contents inside. Each person of the group witnessed in horror as they looked, upon passing, within a box and saw inside a male figure that appeared to writhe in torment, completely covered in a tar-like black substance as Walter had told them. No features could be seen, just a figure covered in tar, writhing constantly. Each box contained a similar writhing blackened figure and the green gas provided the only illumination besides the group's headlamps.

Tam gave out a small shriek upon seeing the first moving figure in the box and asked; "Are they alive? Can we save them?"

Without looking back, Walter replied; "No. Their bodies have decomposed over the decades and only the ichor provides them with form and thought. If we can reverse the flow, we may be able to free their spirits. That is the best we can hope for these poor devils."

"Yeah, and you are the one who created 'these poor devils.' No wonder the Israelis still hunt Nazis. Have you no remorse? Didn't you have any pity when you created these monsters?" said Gareth to Walter.

Walter did not respond, but if the group could have seen his face, they would have seen tears were rolling

Shadowfall

down his cheeks. Walter knew he lacked pity and compassion as a young man. Most young men are that way. It takes age and wisdom to bring them around. Walter felt for his soldiers. He had no idea they were still in anguish all these years, it was almost too much of a strain for him to bear, and he slumped down to his knees.

Tam sensed he was about to fall and never let go, but didn't have time to warn the others. Simon didn't sense it and let go of Tam for only a few seconds, but within that time he got punched and kicked in several locations, and almost couldn't regain his grip on Tam. The moment he did, all action against him ceased. When Simon was getting beat, Gareth had also loosened his grip and received a few shocking blows, but tightened again on Simon and nothing further happened. Levi maintained contact with Gareth at all times and felt nothing save the cold.

Levi spoke next. "It matters not what we feel about Walter. My nation will judge him, and if for some reason he is not, judgement follows in the afterlife. At least that is my belief. We must keep our minds strong and finish this task. It's getting late. Outside it is already the hour of twilight. We cannot allow the citizens of London to experience this invasion of death another night. Tam, help Walter up and let's get moving and remember not to let go of the person in front of you." Tam helped Walter up and the group started moving again. They passed many circular rows of boxes before they came to a clearing. At the clearing, they noted more boxes lay, used to create the spokes of the pentagram, and led right up to the cistern, which was the apex of the Hellish configuration. They stepped into a large clear area between the spokes and proceeded to mount the low rise toward the center.

They walked, still linked together, for a few hundred more feet until they neared the base of the cistern, and could see it fairly clearly in the dim glow that surrounded it. The air was very damp and smelled faintly of rotting meat. The cistern itself appeared to be made of concrete and was about five feet in height. "See! I told you the spear was not in place! It should be directly on top and placed in such a way it points toward the heavens. Since there is no spear, our task should be easy. We just have to..." Whatever else Walter was going to say to the group ended by the sudden appearance of a real flesh and blood man of about middle-age dressed in khaki clothes, holding a spear on top of the concrete structure.

Chapter Seventeen

"**W**er sind Sie?!" bellowed the man from the top of the cistern.

Walter spoke back loudly and plainly. "Ich all dies geschaffen."

"Ach so, Sie müssen Walter Schmitt, Ja?"

"Ja, das ist richtig."

Tam whispered and asked what they were saying. Walter responded to her in English; "He wants to know who we are. He has me figured though. I told him that I was the one who created all of this."

"Und die anderen?"

"Meine freunde. Sie sprechen kein Deutsch."

The man scowled down at Walter a moment and spoke in English.

"Then we will converse in English instead so they can understand. Walter, you were once admired as a great and important man by our Fuhrer, Hitler, and others. It would be a boon to have you return to us as a leader from the past. I do not have time to waste so I will ask only once. Walter, do you and your friends pledge your loyalty and services to the restoration of the Reich?"

Gareth surprised everyone by speaking up first, "Before we can pledge allegiance to anyone, we must first ask who you are?"

Levi whispered in Gareth's ear, "Don't upset this guy. We don't know what he is capable of."

Shadowfall

The man looked toward Gareth and scowled again, seemingly impatient, but answered; "You are impertinent, but also perhaps you are right. My name is Werner Berchtold. I am the last Reichsfuhrer of Germany as appointed by Artur Axmann just before his death in 1996. Does that satisfy you, boy?"

Gareth was unsure what else to say and simply nodded sheepishly. Walter asked the next question. "It was an officer named Hartmann, not Axmann, who last had the spear you are holding. Did you get it from him?"

"No, but I will tell you Colonel Maximillian Hartmann smuggled this spear all the way to Antarctica at the Fuhrer's bidding and hid it there until 1979 when he returned for it. Hartmann brought it all the way back to the Father Land in the hopes of tapping its power and restoring the Reich to former glory. He entrusted this spear to Artur Axmann, the last living member of the party of high rank with this hope.

Unfortunately, neither of them knew how to tap its power until I stepped forward and offered to learn all I could. With funding from the Goebbels estate, I was sent across the globe to learn the arcane knowledge to tap the evil contained within this beast that many call the Spear of Destiny. It took me several years until I was ready to wield it properly.

Over the last few nights, I have been unleashing the power contained within this spear to complete the mission you started Obergruppenfuhrer Schmitt. In your honor I ask you...and your friends...to assist me in completing this glorious work and join the restored Reich. Will you accept?"

Shadowfall

The group remained linked together at hips and shoulders in order to stay connected to Walter. The malevolent shadow figures hovered all around them; raising fists at them and whispering threats.

Walter craned his head back and said to his group, "What should we do or say now?"

Tam asked him in a whisper; "Walter, are you committed to helping us end this?"

"Yes, of course. I am done with my past."

"Then tell him 'No' - from all of us."

Simon heard this and whispered quickly, "No! We should trick him instead to get the spear away from him."

Gareth chimed in too, "There are five of us, and we can quickly overpower him. Say what you want Walter and we can either rush him together or play along with him."

While the others were talking quietly, Levi had taken his right hand off Gareth, still keeping the left one on his shoulder to retain contact, but had managed to take out his gun without notice by anyone. He held it behind Gareth's back, waiting for the right moment.

Walter said, "No more deception. Let us get this done. Prepare yourselves." With this Walter turned back to face Berchtold and said aloud, "My friends and I disagree on some points, but we do agree on one major point. We do not want to join you."

"That is too bad." Berchtold quickly placed the spear into the middle of the cistern and instantly the greenish gas that wafted around the boxes and the pentagram wafted toward it. As the group noticed the change, Berchtold continued to talk as he pulled out a luger pistol from his coat; "The mission will be completed either way. Prepare to die!"

It was Levi that got the first shot off and hit Berchtold in the left shoulder. Gareth had made a movement that threw off his aim from getting Berchtold in the heart. Berchtold went down on one knee and started firing at the group. Panicked, the members let go of their connection to Walter and the shadows, which had been hovering around them, dove in, and attacked.

The group was being hit, kicked, and thrown around. Berchtold had hit Walter, who was now slowly falling to the floor with blood flowing from his chest. Tam was closest to the cistern, ran to it, and made herself into a ball, using its smooth wall to protect her back. Simon was being picked up and thrown around by the shadows. Gareth ran toward Tam to try to cover her with his body, but he was grabbed and hit the whole way. Levi tried to shoot again, but now that the connection was lost, he was being pummeled by his unseen assailants and was nearing unconsciousness.

Berchtold continued firing at the group and hit Levi and Simon. Gareth, Tam, and Walter were too close to the edge of the cistern for Berchtold to get a good shot at them. Blood from wounds inflicted by Berchtold and the undead soldiers was starting to seep and flow from all of the members of the group except Tam. She had no idea why she was not getting attacked and chanced looking up. She saw Walter had crawled to her and was blocking her from attack by raising himself on his arms in front of her. He looked down at her and smiled and said, "At least an old man can still do something gallant for a young woman."

"Walter, you've been shot in the chest!"

"I know. It is getting hard to breathe. I think he got my lung. Tam, you must help me get on top of the cistern without losing contact with me. Once on top maybe one of us can get at Berchtold and the other can dislodge the spear. It may be our only chance."

Tam looked past Walter and saw her friends were getting badly beaten and were sustaining serious injuries. She grabbed at Walter and helped him to stand and grab hold of the edge of the cistern.

Even though he was about to fall unconscious, Levi steeled himself for one last wild shot at Berchtold, which managed to hit him in the right knee, and he went down just as Walter and Tam jumped up on top of the cistern.

Tam had helped Walter up, but now he staggered on his own and pushed Tam behind him as she held his waist. Walter tottered toward the now prone figure of Berchtold who was writhing in pain, mostly from his knee injury. The couple saw the Spear of Destiny was casting a bright green glow and a green ray was emanating from its spear point, out towards the roof of the cavern. The ray was lengthening quickly.

Walter stood above Berchtold and said; "This must end…now. No more blood should be shed in the name of Hitler or Nazis." Berchtold still had the luger in his hand, looked up at Walter and yelled, "Schweinhund!" and proceeded to unload his magazine into Walter's chest. Tam saw what Berchtold was about to do and let go of Walter and threw herself toward the spear. She fell close to it, but it was still not within reach.

From behind her, she heard a low chuckle; she turned and saw Berchtold standing over her, leaning on his left leg to avoid putting pressure on the damaged right leg. He told her, "Your weak, pathetic kind will never win. This is destiny." He raised his right arm to fire the pistol at her, but the gun's chamber clicked empty. He grunted and threw the gun down, took out a knife from his belt and got down on his left knee in front of Tam. She could see a look of demented glee in his eyes and the green reflection glinting off the knife as it started its downward arc. She closed her eyes and screamed.

Tam didn't see Gareth pulling himself up on top of the cistern behind Berchtold. She also missed witnessing Gareth kick Berchtold hard enough to topple him over and dislodge the knife from his grip in doing so; which clattered on the concrete structure and fell off it.

Tam opened her eyes in time to see Gareth jump on top of Berchtold and watched as the two rolled toward the spear. As she watched, shadows were coming towards her quickly. Gareth and Berchtold were now close to the spear. Berchtold reached out to grab it, but Gareth was closer. Gareth grabbed it and managed to dislodge it from its cradle and instantly the green ray disappeared. He yelled, "Tam! Catch!" and threw it as best as he could in her direction. Several shadows tried to grab it as it arced through the air, but it was the one thing, besides Walter, they could not interact with.

Tam, no longer been safe from harm since letting go of Walter, was being hit and kicked. She was getting disoriented by the pummeling, but managed to reach a hand out and grab the spear as it fell next to her. As soon as she gripped it, she no longer felt any attacks as she was connected to it, like she had been with Walter. She didn't know what to do with it, but stood up and went quickly over to Walter.

Gareth and Berchtold were now being ravaged by the spirits of the soldiers who knew no allegiance to either of the living men. Neither man stood a chance of lasting long against their attackers. Both were having their clothes torn and gashes were appearing from where they were clawed at. Black eyes and welts were forming from shadowy punches. The sickening sound of bones being broken could be heard.

Tam knelt down to see if Walter was still alive and found that he was still barely breathing, but blood was trickling from his mouth and his many chest wounds. In a faint wheeze, he told her what had to be done. Tam put the spear in his right hand and Walter closed his eyes and started whispering strange words Tam did not understand. As he did so, the attacks on the others subsided. The power of the punches lessened until they felt like feathers against their skin. After a few more moments, even the feathery sensation dissipated. The attacks were over. Walter stopped whispering and opened his eyes to look at Tam. Walter muttered just a few more words in a low wheeze, closed his eyes, and quit breathing.

Epilogue

The GLIP members had called the number Levi had given them and had been picked up by another team of Mossad operatives that were nearby. The operatives got the survivors out and sealed the remaining entrance with an explosives charge. Tam and Gareth left on the next available flight. Simon remained behind at a local hospital as supposed victim of a 'mugging.' He was lucky that Berchtold's bullet had not fatally harmed him as it had Levi. One of the Mossad operatives was watching over him and told the others his return would happen as soon as he was able to leave. Tam and Gareth split up for their respective homes to get some much-needed rest.

Bleary-eyed Londoners, who had stayed awake all night, were relieved when the morning came and nothing had occurred during the night. Before teatime, there had already been a lot of news coverage about the non-occurrence of last night. Some tuned in for the teatime news at 4 o'clock with Amelia Ainsley.

"Good afternoon London! This is Amelia Ainsley with BBC 1 television. We are here, once again, at the headquarters of the Greater London Investigators of the Paranormal, otherwise known as GLIP. Over the last week, Londoners suffered disturbances credited to ghosts and their manifestations. The confirmed death count stands at 8,365 while the injured count for a number over twice that amount. No one was sure how to label these deaths with any certainty. Some authorities are convinced that some form of terrorist employed gas might have caused the recent mass hysteria and that the deaths may have been self-inflicted. Others suggest that there is indeed some evidence of ghostly apparitions, and, of course, there are countless witnesses to attest to this. Looking for answers, we decided to pay another call to GLIP to see what they can tell us." The camera pans over and Amelia Ainsley joins Tam on-screen. "Tam Winthrop is a senior member of GLIP. Tam, do you have any information regarding the recent disturbances?"

Tam looked into the camera and with a pleasant, but tired, smile said, "No. I have no idea. While we did notice an increase in the amount of paranormal activity as of late, it appears to have stopped."

"Yes, Tam, last night was the first night Londoners were free from what many called a 'ghost invasion.' Do you believe that whatever was happening is finally over?"

"Yes. I personally feel the chaos is over and that everyone will be able to get back on track with their lives."

"Thank you Tam. Londoners are still pouring back into the city and returning to their homes now that local authorities have sounded the all clear. This is Amelia Ainsley for BBC 1 television."

Gareth walked into the GLIP headquarters about an hour later and found all the members of the media were gone. Under his shirt, he had bandages wrapped around his chest and shoulders. He was also wearing sunglasses to keep people from noticing his eyes; blackened and bloodshot. His sore legs caused him to limp too.

Shadowfall

Tam looked up from her laptop just long enough to say, "Hello." Luckily, for Tam, she suffered slight injuries, and did not look at all beaten. Gareth made himself a cup of tea. He was going to ask Tam if she wanted one, but noticed she already had a full cup next to her laptop. He sat down at the table and sipped his tea for a few minutes until Tam finished her typing. She closed her laptop, took a sip of tea, and then smiled at Gareth.

"It took me a few hours this morning and another hour after all those reporters finally left, but I have typed up all of the notes regarding our paranormal investigation. I've written up the Nazi-ghost invasion from beginning to end."

"Tam, it wasn't much of a true investigation. We were not qualified for what we got ourselves into and we are damn lucky to be alive. Besides, you told that cow of a reporter you didn't know anything."

"Let me explain Gareth. I do believe that our expertise in dealing with supernatural manifestations did prepare us to keep clear enough minds to act. Someone not used to dealing with these type of things might have just run out, or might have froze completely and gotten killed. I do believe we may have been more qualified than you might think."

"And what about pleading ignorance to it all?"

Tam gave him a smile and said, "Some things are better left unsaid. Besides, who would believe us? I wouldn't. Nazi-ghosts from World War II? Right...And don't forget what that Mr. Pardo told us."

"Okay. I can buy some of what you say, but I still believe we were damn lucky. I don't trust that Mr. Pardo.

Shadowfall

Look at the situation from my perspective. Both of those Israeli Mossad guys died. Walter Smith...or Nazi Schmitt...or whoever he was also died. Simon is in critical condition at the hospital. You and I were beat up pretty badly. I ended up with two black eyes, several cracked ribs and a broken collarbone. I call sustaining those kinds of injuries as not being that qualified for what we went up against; Lucky, that is what we were...lucky."

Tam smirked a bit and took another sip of her tea before saying, "Perhaps we were a little lucky."

"Hey, you never told me what Walter said to you at the end?"

"Oh, he didn't say much. He told me to place the spear in his hand and then began saying strange things in a language I didn't know, but it didn't sound like German either; maybe Latin? They were his incantations I guess. The very last words he said to me were, "Thank you. I am going home to my beloved Argentina now." I like to think he meant that he was thinking happy thoughts as he passed away."

The two sat in silence for a while longer, sipping their tea.

"Tam, do you think it was right that we destroyed the spear? I mean, it was a Holy relic of some kind. You don't think we should have returned it to the Austrians or something?"

"No. I only held it for a moment, just as you did, but it felt pure evil. I can't explain it, but it felt to me like it was trying to cloud my judgment. It was trying to bend me to its will and make me do bad things. Luckily, I didn't hold it for long. I think burning it was the right thing to do. Hey, did you check on Simon this morning?"

That last sentence from Tam angered Gareth. After all he tried to do to help her on their shared adventure, she still preferred Simon. With a tinge of animosity in his voice he said, "Yeah. He's fine. The doctor said he will be out within a few more days. I guess then you two can go on a date or something."

Tam put down her cup of tea and looked at Gareth with a bewildered look.

"Okay Gareth. Let's have it. Why do you disapprove of Simon so much? I figured you two would be hitting it off by now."

Gareth decided right then to let it all out.

"Simon is okay. It's just that I like you, but I know you prefer Simon. I was hoping we could see each other, but you always bring up Simon. No worries though. I will back off and leave you two alone."

Tam burst out laughing at this.

"It isn't funny Tam!" he yelled.

"Yes it is!" She said between laughing and spitting up tea through her nose. "You silly ass...Simon doesn't like me. He's gay and he told me he fancies you!"

All of a sudden, it all made sense to Gareth; the attention Simon paid him and the talk over at Simon's flat. Gareth was still feeling a bit angry at first, but Tam's laugh was so infectious that he started laughing too.

A few days later, a check arrived from Israel. It was a significant donation made out to The Greater London Investigators of the Paranormal. Since Tam and her team had kept their word of secrecy, Pardo of the Mossad kept his word too.

About the Author

Greg McWhorter resides in Southern California. Since the 1980s, he has worked for newspapers, radio, television, and film. He has been a guest speaker at several universities and the San Diego Comic-Con. Today, McWhorter owns a highly acclaimed record label that specializes in vintage punk rock and hosts a music show for cable TV. Since 1985, McWhorter has been writing crime and horror fiction as well as nonfiction articles on aspects of pop-culture and music. He is a member of the Horror Writer's Association. He can be followed at http://gregmcwhorter.blogspot.com

About the Artist

JORGE AVIÑA

Jorge Avina has been a graphic artist since 1965. He has had the opportunity to work in various print and television projects for national and international media; including illustrations, portraits, comics, character designs, political cartoons, paintings, and story boards for commercials on TV.

For more than 20 years, he has illustrated the covers of "El Libro Vaquero" ("Cowboy Tales"); the most popular printed product of Mexico. "El Libro Vaquero" is a comic about the Wild West, with stories of revenge, betrayal and crime. 70 covers of which were exhibited in the Divus Prager Kabarett in Prague.

Some of his works have been presented at the Musée d'Art Moderne in Paris, Barcelona, London, Switzerland, and Mexico. Roma Publications published a book entitled "Modelling Standard" in Amsterdam, Netherlands. More than 50 illustrations made by Jorge Aviña were included.

Contact information:
jorge_avina@signans.com
www.jorgeavinailustrador.com

Now Available

BONES
EDITED BY JAMES WARD KIRK

Now Available

Made in the USA
Charleston, SC
07 February 2017